THE
BIG
NOTHING

Adrian Fogelin

Ω

PEACHTREE
ATLANTA

Published by
PEACHTREE PUBLISHERS
1700 Chattahoochee Avenue
Atlanta, Georgia 30318-2112

www.peachtree-online.com

FYA
FOG

Cover design by Loraine M. Joyner
Book design by Melanie McMahon Ives

Manufactured in the United States of America
10 9 8 7 6 5 4 3 2 1
First Edition

Library of Congress Cataloging-in-Publication Data

Fogelin, Adrian.
  The big nothing / Adrian Fogelin.-- 1st ed.
    p. cm.
  Summary: A middle-schooler struggles to cope with major family problems, including a brother who might be heading for the Persian Gulf, but finds an escape in piano lessons and the dream of a romance with a popular girl.
  ISBN 1-56145-326-9
  [1. Family problems--Fiction. 2. Music--Fiction. 3. Interpersonal relations--Fiction. 4. Middle schools--Fiction. 5. Schools--Fiction. 6. Iraq War, 2003--Fiction. 7. Tallahassee (Fla.)--Fiction.] I. Title.

  PZ7.F72635Bi 2004
  [Fic]--dc22
                                    2004006327

visit the author's website at
www.adrianfogelin.com

For my friends and neighbors in Seminole Manor.
The stories all begin with you.

Thanks, as always, to the Wednesday Night Writers:
Mary Z. Cox, Richard Dempsey, and Leigh Muller,
and to my sweetheart, Ray Faass.

Congratulations to Arthur Dean Jr. of Sabal Palm Elementary,
winner of the Justin Riggs Cruddy Sneaker Contest.

Dear Duane,

Sorry I sounded weird when you called last night but the Parental Units were right there—Dad in his chair, Mom on the sofa—as far from each other as they could get and still be in the same room. They're doing the not-talking thing again. It keeps me pretty busy.

Dad: Justin, would you please tell your mother she's being paranoid?

Me: Dad says lighten up Mom.

Mom: Justin please inform your father he's a liar.

Me: This is so lame! Would you guys just talk to each other?

Remember those conversations? You used to be the one in the middle. Now all you have to do is march around and shoot guns—want to trade?

I better go. Mrs. Perez is giving me the evil eye like she suspects I'm not doing algebra.

Adios and hasty banana.

Your suffering brother,
Justin

P.S. The units are both off work—Mom said she needed a mental health day but I bet it's backfiring. By the time I get home all that will be left are two pairs of empty shoes with smoke coming out of them.

When I get home from school both of the Units are still alive and hanging out in the kitchen together—things seem to be looking up. Then Dad opens the newspaper with a rattle. "I have a sales trip next week," he says. "I'll be gone a couple days, three max."

Barricaded behind the sports page, Dad doesn't see Mom's worried look. The only thing that gets through to him is The Voice—Mom could pop balloons with that voice. "A sales trip?" she says. "You just got back from the last *sales* trip, Jack."

The alarm goes off in my head: *fight alert...do something...do something.* I quit shoveling my after-school bowl of Coco Puffs into my mouth. "Hey, this is great," I say. "You two are talking to each other!"

It would have gotten a big laugh if my brother Duane had said it.

Mom stares indignantly at the raised newspaper. "This trip wouldn't be to Atlanta, would it?" Without makeup, Mom looks heavier and semi-erased.

Dad doesn't glance up from the page. "There she goes again, Justin, giving me the third degree. Tell her I'm an okay guy."

"Tell her yourself, Dad." I feel like a wishbone getting pulled between them.

"Is the trip to Atlanta or isn't it?" she repeats.

"I confess! I confess!" Dad drops the paper and holds up his hands. "I'm going to Atlanta!" He reaches across the table and pats her hand. "I'm a traveling salesman, hon. I could stay home, but you *do* seem to like to eat."

Mom looks as if he slapped her.

"It was a joke, Kathy. A joke. Don't be so sensitive."

"I'm going out," I announce.

"Hey," Dad calls after me, "don't leave me alone with this crazy woman!"

The screen bangs shut behind me. That was a cheap shot about Mom liking to eat, but she was nagging him. She's always nagging him.

Up until two weeks ago, at this point in a fight, I'd be out of here. In less than a minute I'd be knocking on Ben Floyd's door. We'd play video games, listen to music—no one ever yells at his house. But all of a sudden everything's different. My best friend has a girlfriend. He's probably over at Cass's right now, sitting on the couch with her and her sister, watching Oprah.

"All you do is lie to me!" Mom's voice soaks through the screen. She's crying now, definitely. I sit down on the porch steps.

"There goes that overactive imagination of yours again," Dad says, and he laughs.

I pull my head down between my shoulders. I hate it when he laughs at her.

Maybe if I yell that the house is on fire they'll stop. Maybe if I start bleeding a whole lot…. I can practically hear my brother: *Great plan, Jus. Bleed to death, that'll stop 'em.*

I wish I'd gone up to his old room and closed the door. Nothing gets to me there.

"Who is she this time, Jack?"

"Nobody," says Dad. "After a day with customers I'm bushed. I go to the motel and turn on the tube."

Dad sells supplies and equipment to mom-and-pop restaurants. Seems like half the time he lives at a Motel 6. When he comes in from a sales trip, he kicks off his shoes and shouts, "Jack is back!" When we were young, Duane and I would pound down the stairs and jump on him. Mom would too.

I don't know when things changed, but they did.

Since Duane enlisted, Dad's away more than ever. When he is here all Mom does is give him the third degree about the girlfriends he supposedly has on the road.

In the wedding picture on Dad's dresser, Mom looks hot, but she's put on the pounds since then. Dad's tall and he's still really built—he's also bald, but on him, bald works. I can see why she gets jealous. But does he mess around? No way. Dad is just a friendly guy.

I drum my hands quietly on the step on either side of me.

"Nobody, huh?" Mom sounds less weepy, more ticked. "Then explain *this!*"

Suddenly, there's a third voice coming from inside the house. Mom's playing a message on the answering machine: exhibit A. I can't make out the words, but I don't have to. She's always confronting him with bogus stuff like a smudge of lipstick that's really ketchup, a whiff of perfume that's just deodorizer from the latest motel.

I drum a little faster.

"Well?" Mom says when the message ends. "I'm waiting, Jack." Then she repeats, at the top of her lungs, "I'm waiting!"

I don't want to be here any more. I've had enough. It's time to go away.

To get where I'm going I don't even have to stand up. I just focus on the rhythm I'm drumming and hunt for ways to make it more elaborate. If it's complex enough I can climb inside it and sort of disappear. I get a little help. Someone I can't see is running in the street. I play my rhythm against the slap of sneakers.

I time my breathing so it matches every fourth step. Breathe in on four, out on four; in on four, out on four. The front yard blurs. The exact moment I drain out of the me who cares and pour into The Big Nothing is like the second between being awake and asleep; it's hard to pinpoint. But as soon as it happens, the Battle of the Units fades to a fuzzy *blah-blah-blah.*

Ladies and gentlemen, Justin Riggs has just left his body.

I've almost forgotten that the *slap-slap* is a pair of running feet when Jemmie Lewis flashes by. I only see her for a second as she passes the gap where the path cuts through the hedge that surrounds our yard.

"Hey, Big Rig!" She skips backwards a few steps and reappears. Her skinny ribs heave. She breathes through her mouth. When she leans forward to rest her hands on her thighs, the belly button below the edge of her crop top winks.

"You warm enough?" I call to her. "It *is* January."

"This is Florida, Big." She trots up the walk, her dark skin slick with sweat. "Besides, anyone moving as fast as me generates a lot of heat." She grabs the rail and does a couple of deep knee bends. Her cornrows zig and zag like lightning bolts. I don't know why she stopped, but I hope she runs off before the Units fire up again.

She flops down a couple of steps below me. "You're awful quiet, Big."

This is weird. Unless you count arguing over the score in a pickup game, I don't think I've ever had a real conversation with Jemmie Lewis. Jemmie is Cass's friend, Cass is Ben's friend, and Ben is my friend. So what does that make Jemmie and me? Friends twice removed?

5

And why is she calling me "Big" all of a sudden? Because I'm not—at least in the vertical sense.

She rests her pointy elbows on the top stair and leans back. Why is she getting comfortable?

"Shouldn't you be running with Cass?" I ask.

"I don't always run with Cass," she says, scratching her knee.

"Sure you do." Until Ben and Cass hooked up, the girls were inseparable.

She scratches her kneecap like she wants to draw blood. "Well, where's your best buddy Ben?"

"I don't always hang with Ben," I say.

"Sure you do."

Something smashes inside the house.

Jemmie rolls her eyes my way. "What was that?"

"TV show."

She pops to her feet and claps twice. "Come on, let's run!"

"Uh…no thanks." The only one who can keep up with Jemmie is Cass, and she's with Ben, watching Oprah. "You go right ahead, though. Don't let me hold you up."

She thrusts out a hip and rests her knuckles on it; she taps her foot. She's doing her black girl, don't-mess-with-me thing. The easiest way to get along with Jemmie is to go along—but my running sucks. I notice the wheels of my skateboard poking out of the tall grass. "Okay, okay." I stand and casually flip the board with a toe.

Wheels, it turns out, are pretty cool. Within fifty yards I'm smoking Jemmie-the-flash.

I slow a little and a hand clamps my belt. The *zizzzz* of the wheels changes pitch as she hops on the back of the board.

Jemmie is one of the top five popular girls in our class. Why would she risk being seen riding with a guy who looks like the Pillsbury Doughboy with zits?

When Dad passed down the good-looks genes, my brother got them all. I could run around with straws up my nose or set myself on fire. No self-respecting girl would notice me, especially not a girl like Jemmie. But I don't mind her hanging on the back of my belt. I could get used to it.

We circle the block. We've just pulled even with the gap in our hedge when the door flies open and a pair of Dad's golf shoes sails out. Tongues flapping, they tumble down the steps.

I drag my foot and we lurch to a stop. Jemmie thumps into my back. "What's going on?" she asks, hopping off the board. She points at the shoes on the lawn.

The shoes are followed by a nine iron and Duane's ancient cat, Gizmo, who darts out the open door. The cat skims the ground like a shadow. The nine iron nearly beans him as he breaks for the bushes.

Jemmie raises an eyebrow. "TV?"

"Reality TV." I plant a foot on the sidewalk and shove off as hard as I can.

"Would you cool it, Big? Would you just slow down?" I hear Jemmie running flat-out, but I keep right on kicking the board forward. Watching Dad's junk land on the lawn makes me want to barf.

I feel a jerk as she grabs my belt and jumps on again. Riding together, we careen down the hill and sail around the corner onto Roberts Avenue. We almost get hit by a guy backing out of his driveway.

○

We lace our fingers through the chain link. "This is pitiful," I huff. "Out of all the places in the world, we end up here."

On the other side of the fence is the school basketball court.

Past that is Monroe Middle School, the place where we just finished wasting the day.

Jemmie steps off the back of the board. "We could go somewhere else."

"Like where?"

"USA store?"

"You have any money on you?" I ask.

"No."

"Me neither."

"Cemetery? Cass and I go there sometimes."

"Nah." Ben and I go to the cemetery too. We play this game called "Dead-Guy Baseball." The only equipment needed is a Superball, and I have one in my pocket, but Jemmie would probably think it was stupid.

"Wanna sit?" she asks. We walk onto the court and press our backs against the fence. The wire creaks as we slide down.

"Hey, chain link is kind of comfortable," I say after a while. "Like a lawn chair."

Note to self: Quit talking.

She picks up a pebble and scrapes a wavy white line onto the blacktop. "Wish we had a basketball."

"Yeah, me too." Sure I do. When we play pickup games, the girls beat the guys more than half the time. One-on-one, she'd cream me.

I listen to her breathe. Why is she staring at my feet?

"Nice kicks," she says.

"Oh, yeah. It took me years to get 'em just right." My sneakers are so blown that my socks pooch out the sides. But the leg situation is worse than the shoes. Hers are a good three inches longer than mine. I'd like to point out to her that her height is all in her legs, that she's only about an inch taller than me.

She has to bend her knee to nudge the toe of my sneaker with hers. "You miss Ben?" she asks.

"Yeah, I guess." I slide down on my tail. My legs get longer. "You miss Cass?"

"No." She jerks her knees up and hugs them with her skinny arms. "I'm mad at her. I mean, *I'm* her best friend, not him. I'd never dump her if I got a boyfriend. Would you dump Ben for a girl?"

"Uhh..." I try to imagine me with a girl.

"I *know* you wouldn't," she says.

I'm still trying to imagine myself with a girl when Cass trots up, ponytail swinging. "There you are, Jemmie!" Her sneakers squeak to a stop. "I've been looking for you *every*where! Oh, hi, Justin."

Jemmie stares at a cut on Cass's shin. "Thought your dad didn't let you shave."

Cass tucks one pale, freckly leg behind the other. "Lou says guys don't like hairy legs. She lent me her razor." I blush. Do girls usually talk about shaving their legs in front of guys? It's like I'm not here.

"Since when have you ever listened to your ditsy sister? Going with Ben is making you crazy, girl! You're changing so fast I don't even know you."

"All I did was shave my legs! Come on, Jemmie," Cass pleads. "Let's run like we always do, okay?" But Jemmie doesn't answer. "Jemmie...are you mad at me?"

Jemmie jumps to her feet. I'm thinking *girl fight*, but instead of laying into Cass, Jemmie sprints toward the track. Cass chases after her.

"Nice talking to you," I shout as they shrink in the distance. "I'm going now. Catch you later." I go the long way to Ben's, bypassing my street.

○

Ben and I lounge, our necks resting against the top of the front seat of a pink Cadillac we call the Pimpmobile—at least when his dad isn't listening.

"Were the girls getting along okay?" Ben asks.

"When I left, they were running." He nods, then we both stare through the P-mobile's windshield at the junkers that crowd the Floyds' backyard.

Junker is our term too. Ben's dad, who teaches auto mechanics at the high school, prefers the term "Vehicles of Promise."

My brother Duane spent lots of Saturdays and after-school hours here, messing with cars. The blue Camaro with one green door parked next to the tree used to be his. He could've given it to me—I'll have my permit in a year and a half. Instead he sold it to a guy named Marcus. I notice that the windows are taped. "Is Marcus going to paint it?" I ask Ben.

"Yeah," Ben says. "He's gonna do it in gold flake."

"That'll be tacky."

The truth is, as long as the car stays the same, I can almost see Duane out there in a greasy T-shirt, his head under the hood. I'll probably freak when the green door goes.

Ben cranks the radio all the way up, then tosses a piece of microwave popcorn into the air. It bounces off the head liner before he catches it in his mouth. "Two points," he shouts over the pounding rap on the radio.

"What's the deal?" I ask, digging into the bag. "Two points if it rebounds, one for an air shot?"

O

By the time the setting sun touches the wiper blades, Ben's beating me by thirty-seven points. The clock on the dash says six-twenty. The Floyds eat at six-thirty on the dot.

Maybe he'll invite me.

"Ben?" his mom calls from the back door. "Ben, honey, Cass is on the phone. Be quick. Supper's ready."

"Girlfriends," he grumbles. "They never leave you alone." But he's out of the car in a heartbeat. I call, "See ya, Ben-honey," as he sprints to the house.

Skating home I catch a stone with my back wheel and go down on my butt. Could the day get any better? I kick the board up and carry it the rest of the way. It's getting dark.

I slide through the gap in the hedge and scope out the situation. No shoes on the lawn, no golf clubs.

As I cross the yard something glints in the grass. I bend down and pick up one of Dad's cuff links. I straighten and notice that the Town Car is gone, only Mom's rust-bucket Corolla is in the driveway. They're probably at AJ's Sports Bar having a beer, or maybe they're out for supper; they do stuff like that after a fight. I cram the cuff link into my pocket.

I'm about to fish the key out of the fake gas lamp on the wall, but I try the door on the off chance they forgot to lock up. It swings open. There's no note from Mom on the coffee table either. The Units are getting slack.

Inside, all the lights are out. The living room looks as murky as the bottom of the sea—just the conditions Duane used to look for when he wanted to mess with my mind. *See that movement behind the couch, Jus?*

My brother had me convinced there were ninjas back there in the dark.

He wasn't always out to scare me. We did all kinds of stuff together, like wrestling and watching the tube. Once he got the Camaro, we rode around, me in the back, one of his buddies, like Craig or Diesel, riding shotgun.

Duane planned to go to college on a baseball scholarship. Three or four schools scouted him, but his grades were lousy.

The closest he got to higher education was a job on the grounds crew at FSU. One afternoon, a recruiter named Frank called. He wasn't with a college ball team, he was with the Army. Duane signed anyway.

He wrote me every day when he was in Basic, no lie. I thought he was crazy, but he said he missed home. Ne never admitted he was scared but I could tell he was. He wrote me about belly-crawling across a pit in the pitch-dark, M60s firing a whisker above his butt. *The Army doesn't mess around*, he said.

Now he's finishing his MOS. That's Army for Military Occupational Specialty. When he's done, he'll be a Light-Wheel Vehicle Mechanic—specialty 63B.

The slacker hardly ever writes anymore, but he calls home every Monday night. Last night he bragged about what great shape he was in. *I could whip your little butt, bro, one arm tied behind my back.*

Oh, yeah? I said, *Come on home and try it.*

I sure would like to see him.

Right now would be good. If he were here he'd take charge of supper. He'd fix chicken fingers à la cheese sauce, or egg rolls on a bed of French fries, maybe macaroni dogs. If the fridge was empty, Duane and I would hit the golden arches or Taco Bell.

I do a drop-and-roll over the arm of the recliner and grab the remote, thinking I'll solve the food problem later. I hit the On button. But the loudest sound I hear doesn't come from the tube; it's The Voice. "Turn that noise off!" Startled, I chuck the remote into the air. It hits the corner of the coffee table and the TV goes off.

"Mom?"

She's sitting in the half-dark kitchen, hands flat on the table like she's waiting for nail polish to dry, only it's too dark to polish nails. I flip the light switch. She keeps staring at her hands. "C'mon, Mom. Don't go zombie on me."

I unplug myself when things are bad, but her Big Nothing is way bigger than mine. She doesn't even blink. Right now, she is so not-there that it's hard to believe the squawk about the TV came from her.

I wave a hand in front of her eyes. "Earth to Mom."

"He's gone," she finally says, tears piling up against her lower lids. "Gone for good." The tears begin to spill.

I hand her a paper towel. "He's on a sales trip, Mom. He'll be back." She stares at the towel. "Blow, Mom." She honks her nose. "That's better, isn't it? Hey, I know something that'll cheer you right up. Pizza rolls!" I stick my head in the freezer.

Mom blows her nose again. "Her name is Susan. She lives in Atlanta."

I breathe out hard and the cold air in the ice cavern swirls around me. This is a first. Mom's suspicions have never had names before—let alone hometowns. Her imagination is *really* working overtime.

"Sorry, Mom. No pizza rolls. The only thing in here is dinosaur steak."

Her chair creaks. "Dinosaur steak?"

"Got to be. It's been in the freezer so long it's glacierized. Let's go out and get something."

Mom shakes the box of Coco Puffs I left on the table.

I take it out of her hand and put it back in the cabinet. "I'm thinking cheeseburgers."

She dabs her eyes with a corner of the towel. "That woman had the nerve to call and leave a message on my machine: *'Jack? Call Susan as soon as you can, okay? I'll be at the Atlanta number.'*"

"Don't worry, Mom. I bet this Susan person's, like, seventy years old with popped-out veins. She probably wanted an extra order of salad forks." I take her sweater off the back of the chair and guide her arms into the sleeves. "Just go easy on Dad when he gets home again. Be nice to him, okay? Now, can we make that burger run?"

I grab her by the elbows and steer her toward the door. She shuffles along like she's suddenly come down with a terminal disease. When we pull even with the coffee table I snag her car keys and press them into her hand. "Here, Mom. You might want these."

Dear Duane,

   Dad's gone AWOL—he split Tuesday night. The fight was major. Mom went crazy and tossed his stuff out on the lawn. He hasn't even called. I'm not worried—I know Dad—but Mom's so bummed she can't get out of bed. I had to call her in sick a couple days last week.
   What can I say except wish you were here. I sure could use your help bro.

                              Justin

P.S. I tried to stop the fight, but they don't listen to me. Fight-stopping is your specialty.

Our mailbox is being swallowed by the hedge, which hasn't been pruned since my family moved here. I scratch my arm up putting the letter in the box, even though mailing it is pointless. Tomorrow is Monday, Duane's phone-home night. I'll tell him all about the Battle of the Units then.

Sometimes I write him just to get stuff out of my head.

As I walk back, my stomach lets out a multidecibel rumble. I forgot to put that in the letter: *P.S. Serious lack of foodage.*

We've been eating whatever we had around. I chipped the dinosaur steak out of the freezer the night before last and nuked it in the microwave until the ice crystals melted off. Then I fried it, like, half an hour on a side. It got kind of tough. I put half on a plate for Mom. She wasn't hungry, so I ate both halves. To disguise the funny freezer taste I ate a pile of pickles.

Since then it's been canned spaghetti and cold cereal all the way—but now we're pretty much out of anything remotely edible.

I wouldn't mind a free school breakfast about now, even though my friend Leroy says they're mostly flabby white bread and pink cereal. I could always walk down to the USA Store, but unless you're after pork rinds or Little Debbies, the choices aren't great there either.

"Mom," I shout as I come back inside. "We need to go to the grocery store." I lope up the stairs and breeze into her room. I snap the curtains open. "Wakey, wakey."

As she burrows deeper into the bed, she sends out a muffled command. "Go. To. School."

"Sorry to inform you, Mom, but it's Sunday."

"Then go away."

I sit down on the edge of the bed and jangle the car keys. "Come on, Mom. About all that's left in the house is a jar of mayo and a box of saltines. The Giz and I are starving."

Mom plays dead.

I whisper, "Don't do this to me, Mom." I feel dumb for sounding scared. This isn't the first time Dad's checked out for a few days. It's just that Mom seems worse than usual. Time to retreat and regroup.

When I get downstairs, I take a quick glance out the living room window. One of these times, as long as the cosmic forces don't know that I care, Dad's car will be parked over the oil stain on the driveway.

But not this time.

I ask myself, What would Duane do? He'd fix Mom a cup of coffee. He'd try again.

"Wake up and smell the coffee, Mom!" I wave a hand over the mug, hoping the smell of instant Maxwell House can penetrate pillow. "One hundred percent Co-*lum*-bian. Good to the last drop."

She lifts the corner of the pillow. One eye shows. "Justin…please…please…leave me alone."

"Can't do it. Got to keep you out of the black hole." I try to whip the covers back, but the fingers on the edge of the blanket are hanging on tight. Mom may be too depressed to get out of bed, but she isn't getting weak.

"Leave me alone, Jus. We'll go later."

I drop the blanket. "When is later, Mom? This afternoon? Tomorrow? Next Thursday? The Fourth of July? We'll all starve to death before you think it's later!" I shut the door behind me and press my back against it.

Got to calm down. No need to panic. It's not like anything

terrible has happened. Mom won't get out of bed and we need food, that's all.

I find her purse and extract some bucks. I'm stuffing the cash into the pocket of my shorts when I feel something hard at the bottom: Dad's cuff link. I don't know why, but I've been moving it from pocket to pocket every time I change my pants. Today I'm in shorts because everything winter-appropriate is dirty. I fish the cuff link out. His initials, *JRR*, squiggle across the shiny gold rectangle.

The cuff links were Dad's reward for being salesman of the year for his region. Once I heard Mom accuse him of getting them from one of his "girlfriends." I can sort of understand why he takes a break now and then.

I jam the salesman-of-the year cuff link back in my pocket between Mom's twenties. Now I have cash, but Publix is a couple of miles away. I decide to bike over—but I can't carry much without baskets, so I improvise.

I empty my pack onto the sofa and put it on, but when I climb on the bike, my front tire is soft. Bummer. I think for a second. Ben has a pump. I could walk the bike over to his house and pump up the tire. His bike has baskets, and maybe he'd come along—but Cass is probably there, so forget it. I let the bike fall over on the lawn.

I throw my backpack on the kitchen table and grab Mom's reject cup of coffee—plus the saltines and mayonnaise—and carry them out to the porch. I sit on the top step, faithful cat at my side. The Giz leans against my leg, sharing warmth. Giz is fourteen. A big gust would blow him away like a burger wrapper. His gray-striped coat is as loose as the formerly fat guy's pants on the I-lost-a-hundred-pounds commercial.

I take one sip of Mom's coffee and spit it out. "Projectile vomiting!" I shout at the cat. It's my favorite term from health class, but Giz doesn't look impressed. I yank the shoulder of my T-shirt up and wipe my mouth. "Why does anyone drink this stuff?" It might be less toxic with milk and sugar—but the sugar bowl's empty, and our milk is pretty expired.

I hang onto the mug anyway; it keeps my hands warm. "A major cold front must have come through during the night, Giz. I feel like my butt is about to drop off." I unroll one of the newspapers that have been piling up all week and sit on it. Holding my nose, I take a big swallow from the mug, hoping to warm myself from the inside out. I chase it with a mayo-saltine sandwich.

I fix the Giz a mayonnaise cracker and set it on the step. He licks the cracker clean—he doesn't have enough teeth left to deal with anything crunchy. He arches as I run a hand over his skinny ribs, then his ears swivel forward and he goes tense. "What's the matter, Giz?"

There it is again, the sound of a single runner approaching. This time when Jemmie pops into the gap in the hedge she stops. It's like she expects to see me. She wears sweats and a knit cap in Florida A&M orange and green. The cold air is cloudy with her breath. "Hey, Big Rig! Are you trying to catch your death?"

She got that "catch your death" right out of her grand-mother's mouth. According to Nana Grace, folks can "catch their death" in all kinds of ways. Sitting on a freezing porch in a T-shirt, shorts, and bare feet has to be near the top of her list.

"What are you and Gizmo eating?" Jemmie asks, shaking out her arms.

"Nothing."

She dashes up the steps and turns the jar with the toe of her sneaker. "Crackers and mayonnaise? That's kind of pitiful."

"Don't knock it 'til you've tried it." I slather a saltine, slap a second cracker on top, and hand it to her. She takes a teeny bite. "Not that bad, is it?"

She tosses the saltine sandwich over the railing.

"Hey, don't waste it! Some of us think they're okay."

"Come to my house if you want something that's *really* okay. Nana Grace just put a batch of biscuits in the oven."

"Biscuits?" I almost drool. "Sure." But I'm not sure. Me in Jemmie Lewis's house without Ben, Cass, and the others? Then I picture biscuits on a plate. They call to me. "Sure," I repeat with more conviction. "Let's go."

"Shouldn't you tell someone where you're going first?" Then she looks at my clothes like she knows I slept in them. "Shouldn't you change?"

I snatch the cat up so he won't get left out in the cold. "Be right back. You stay here, my Mom's sick." I don't want her to come inside. The house is pretty trashed.

I consider changing, but into what? There are no clean pants, no clean socks either. I fish my sneaks out from under the couch with my toes and jam my feet in them. The hole in the left one's getting so bad my little toe sticks out like a grub.

I find my down jacket crunched into a corner of the sofa—I used it as a pillow while watching a *Twilight Zone* Marathon. Before I go I open the expired carton of milk and smell it. It smells pretty okay. I empty it into a bowl for Giz. A dog would drink the milk even if it was bad and get sick, but Giz won't. Cats can tell the difference.

"I'm going out," I shout toward the bedroom. I wait with my hand on the banister, but Mom doesn't answer. "Okay. See ya later."

○

"Why, Justin Riggs," says Nana Grace. "So nice to see you." Jemmie's grandmother stands at the stove, butter popping in a skillet, a brown egg in each hand. Most of the time she wears a housedress, but I figure she's just come home from early church. Under her apron is a shiny blue dress with pink flowers. The feathers on her hat flutter as she shakes her head. "You'll catch your death running around in shorts in this weather."

Jemmie is giving me a told-you-so look when her mother calls, "Jemmeal? You left your church shoes in the middle of the living room floor! Run them upstairs right this minute."

"Yes, ma'am." I hear Jemmie take the stairs two at a time.

Nana cracks the eggs and adds them to the mixing bowl. Humming, she whips the eggs and dumps them in the pan. "Glad you're here," she says over her shoulder. "You think you can help us eat some of this food?"

The kitchen smells so good, I have to swallow my spit before I can answer. "Sure, be glad to."

She nods toward the sink. "Care to wash your hands?" I figure that means I should. I'm drying my hands when Jemmie lopes back into the kitchen. "Jemmie," says Nana, turning her by her shoulder. "Go get your brother. Justin'll help me carry."

Basket of biscuits in one hand, platter of bacon in the other, I follow Nana Grace to the dining room. Nana's carrying the eggs and grits. A spread like this would be Christmas breakfast at my house. Any other morning we raid the fridge and cupboards—Dad calls it foraging.

Jemmie lugs Artie into the dining room. She plops him in his booster seat, then pries a truck out of his hand. "No trucks at the table," she says, putting it on the sideboard behind him.

Nana Grace touches the chair across from Jemmie. "Sit here, Justin." She sits at one end of the table with Artie at her elbow;

Mrs. Lewis sits at the other. Nana Grace asks everyone to bow their heads. Then, even though they just got home from church, they all start to pray.

I stare at my own face reflected in my china plate. I hope this won't take too long—I'm starving, and the lace tablecloth is tickling my bare knees.

While Nana Grace thanks God for each thing we're about to eat, I sneak a look around the table—and catch Artie reaching for his truck. He pulls his hand back like I'm going to yell at him. But I wink. I don't have a problem with trucks at the table.

I scan the family gathering and think, what's missing from this picture? No father figure. The Lewises moved in a couple of summers ago. In that whole time I've never heard word one about a Mr. Lewis.

As messed up as my family is, at least I have a dad.

"Amen," they chorus. "And pass the grits," adds Jemmie.

I shovel half a dozen giant forkfuls of eggs into my mouth before I remember that I'm not at home in front of the TV. I look around, afraid I'm about to be busted by the manners police. Even Artie's eating neater than me. But no one seems to have noticed. Jemmie's mom is nibbling fruit salad and a piece of dry whole-wheat toast. She's reading the folded newspaper beside her plate. "President Ponders War," says the upside-down headline. Jemmie is stirring a gob of butter into her grits.

"What's up with you, Artie?" I say, remembering that good manners include making polite conversation.

"I'm this many." He holds up three fingers.

"Three big ones. That's pretty old." That's enough polite conversation. I take a few small bites, then go back to stuffing my face.

"My, my," says Nana Grace. Mouth full, I glance up. The

corners of her eyes are bunched in a million wrinkles. "You *do* have a healthy appetite," she says, sliding more bacon onto my plate. "A cook couldn't ask for no better compliment."

I compliment her until I'm so stuffed I can hardly breathe. I drop the fork with a clatter. "Nana Grace," I groan, "you saved my life."

"In that case, it's payback time. Come on in the kitchen. I'll wash, you dry."

At my house we wash as needed, but if Nana Grace wants to go all out, hey, I'm glad to help.

She hums as she runs hot water into the sink. "Can I dry too?" Jemmie begs. "Pleeeeease."

Nana Grace flicks her with a towel, then passes the towel to me. "You shoo on outta here and practice your piano. Make your mama happy." Jemmie mopes off. I hear the lid of the piano bang open.

Nana shakes her head over Jemmie's plate and sighs. "I hate to waste, but you may as well scrape this into the garbage, Justin." I dump the cold eggs, but sneak the bacon into the pocket of my shorts for the Giz.

I'm not real experienced when it comes to drying dishes, but Nana Grace isn't hard to keep up with because she keeps stopping to listen to her granddaughter play. "Mercy sake, don't beat it to death, Jemmeal," she calls out. "Make it sing."

Jemmie just plays louder.

Nana fishes a glass out from under the suds, then rolls her eyes. "I hope you ain't hearin' this, Marvin." I turn around to see who she's talking to, but I'm the only one in the room.

While waiting for incoming dishes, I play along with Jemmie on the edge of the counter. Sometimes it seems as if the notes should go slower. Other times, I wish she'd pick it up a little. Jemmie plays as if she's typing a report.

We're playing right together when a voice says, "You play?"

I whip my hands off the counter. "Play what?" I ask. Nana Grace is standing by the sink holding a drippy glass. "You mean the piano?" I take the glass out of her hand. "I don't play anything musical," I say, which is not exactly true. I have this plastic recorder from the fourth-grade recorder band I mess around on sometimes when I'm alone. "The only thing I play is basketball, and I stink at it. Ask Jemmie."

She feels around in the dishwater for the next glass. "Maybe you'd be better at piano."

"I doubt it. I'm mediocre to bad at most things."

"Won't know unless you try." She holds a tumbler up to the window to inspect it. "Now, I don't read music. I play by ear. But I could get you started."

"Nah, that's okay." I know I couldn't do it. Especially if Jemmie was listening.

Mrs. Lewis comes into the kitchen pressing her temples the way Mom does when a migraine is kicking up. "Is that list ready?"

"Hangin' on the icebox," says Nana Grace.

Mrs. Lewis slides the list out from under a magnet. "Butter, Mom? How about a low-cholesterol substitute?"

"Ain't no substitute for butter," says Nana Grace, turning the tap off hard.

"Wait—is someone going to the grocery store?" I ask. I still have the money from Mom's purse in my pocket.

"Uh-huh." Mrs. Lewis tucks the list in her purse. "I'm going to Publix."

"Mind if I ride along? I need to pick up a few things. My dad's on the road and Mom isn't feeling well."

"Oh?" Mrs. Lewis glances up from the list. "Any way I can help?"

Jemmie's mom is a nurse. She's always visiting families in the neighborhood that don't have insurance, like my friend Leroy and his brother Jahmal. "Don't get sick around her," Leroy warns. "She'll make you strip down to your drawers." But I have the feeling that Mom is a kind of sick Mrs. Lewis wouldn't understand.

"She has a cold," I lie. "Nothing serious."

In the car, I catch her staring at the grease stain seeping through my pocket. I cross my legs to block her view. I just hope she doesn't smell bacon.

We separate at Publix, grab carts, and go. Mrs. Lewis starts at the beginning: produce.

The theme from *Goldfinger* is being piped into the aisles. *Dah-dah, dah-daaaaaa, Goldfinger!* I put a foot on the bottom of the cart and blast off, leaving Jemmie's mom squeezing cantaloupes.

An old lady wheeling a load of cat food lets out a screech as I maneuver around her. "Thanks for the reminder," I say, veering toward the shelves and grabbing three jumbo cans of Kitty Please.

In the next aisle I weave between two girls in FSU sweatshirts. The one on the left jumps back. "Where'd you learn to drive?"

Two aisles away I drag a toe and bring the cart to a stop in frozen foods. While I fill the cart with the essentials—tacos, pizza rolls, chicken nuggets, and Popsicles—I hum a note that harmonizes with the thrum of the big freezer; like the AC at home, it plays a note I can hang a tune on.

I'm reaching for a box of Texas toast when Jemmie's mother wheels around the corner. While she consults her list, I check out the contents of her cart: broccoli, oranges, yogurt, skim milk, whole-wheat crackers—it's like she has the surgeon general riding around inside her head telling her what to get. Nana Grace's butter is all by itself in the far corner of the cart, as if it's been sent to time out.

Mrs. Lewis glances up, takes one look at my cart, and her inner surgeon general goes ballistic. "Your mom must have been too sick to make a list. I *know* she wouldn't want you to eat all this junk." And she begins putting stuff back.

I could say, Yeah, my mom lets me eat junk 24-7, but that would be like saying she's a bad parent. Mom's tired and distracted, and right now she's seriously horizontal, but Mom is okay.

O

"Mom?" I stand in the middle of the kitchen hugging two full grocery bags. "You awake?" I hear a groan and the creak of bedsprings from upstairs as she rolls over. I set the bags down and dig the change out of my pocket: eleven dollars and twenty-four cents. I smooth the bills out and lay them on the table, then arrange the coins in a smiley face.

Now what? I want to fix Mom some lunch, but the food Mrs. Lewis picked for me isn't food you can heat and eat. You have to do all kinds of stuff to it.

What you need is a nice lean chicken for soup, she'd said, picking one out for me.

What does a chicken in a plastic bag have to do with soup? Soup comes in cans. All the food Jemmie's mother made me buy is like that—ingredients, not meals.

The Giz walks figure eights around my legs, meowing hopefully, which reminds me. "Hey, Giz, brought you something." I fish the strips of bacon out of my pocket, tear a couple into little pieces, and put them in his dish. I chew on the third cold strip and start unpacking.

"What to feed Mom…what to feed Mom." Down at the bottom of bag one, I see a jar of peanut butter. "All right! I can do peanut butter!" Bag two holds a loaf of bread. But when I open the jar, a lake of oil is floating on top. "What the—?" Then I read the label. It says "natural old-fashioned."

"Just what Mom needs, a good old-fashioned slime sandwich." I dump the oil down the sink and scoop out a gob of what's underneath. When I go to put the sandwich on a napkin, the peanut butter is kind of oozy. I wash and dry a plate, set the sandwich on it, and cut the sandwich in half diagonally, the way Mom likes.

I rub an apple on my T-shirt until it's nice and shiny.

Hands full, I use my butt to push open Mom's door. I slide in, carrying the plate. "Mom?" She's just a soft mound beneath the covers. Gizmo, who is basically a floor cat, sinks his claws into the bedspread and pulls himself up like a mountain climber. He curls up in the crook of her knees.

She doesn't groan. She doesn't twitch. "Lunchtime, Mom. I made you the specialty of the house. PB sandwich. Sorry, we were all out of J."

Mom rises slowly from the covers and rests her back against the headboard. Her hair is flat on one side and sticking out on the other, a serious case of bed-head. But I don't laugh. I set the plate on top of the covers and wait. She picks up half a sandwich, then takes a tiny bite. "You want something to drink with that? I have OJ and skim milk."

"Milk would be nice."

"Moo juice coming right up."

O

Mom gets out of bed but doesn't dress, except to put on a robe and slippers. She scuffs down to the kitchen and dumps most of the sandwich in the trash.

"Mom...you really need to eat."

She pours the milk in Giz's bowl and opens the fridge. "I thought you said—"

"Mrs. Lewis took me shopping. I told her you were sick. She said a nice chicken soup would make you feel better. You don't know how to make chicken soup, do you?"

She pushes the sleeves of the robe up to her elbows. "Grams used to make it. I think I remember how." She lowers her arms and the sleeves slide back down.

"Hey, great!" I was still eating baby food when Grams died, but Mom says she was a great cook. I never thought any of it rubbed off on Mom, though. "Tell me what to do," I say. "We'll make chicken soup right now."

She pushes her hair off her forehead with her wrist. "I think the first step is to boil the chicken."

I find a big pot, fill it with water, and plop in the bird, but it floats. When I push it under, it pops back up. "Looks like a fat man in a swimming pool, doesn't it, Mom? Take a look, it's pretty funny." But by the time she drags herself over, it just seems lame.

While we wait for the bird to get soupable, Mom pops a Fred Astaire–Ginger Rogers movie into the VCR. Mom has a collection of black-and-white films. They were old even when she was a kid, but she loves watching them. According to her the world was more civilized back when women wore white gloves and men wore fedora hats. If I don't have anything else to do I watch with her. The fedora guys have some smooth moves.

Take Fred. Fred doesn't seem to know he's a skinny dork with a big head. When he puts the moves on Ginger (the blond babe), it works.

"You know," says Mom, stroking the Giz, who is curled up

against her side, "Ginger couldn't even dance when he chose her as his partner."

"Then why did he pick her?" I ask, like we've never had this conversation before.

"Just look at them!" Ginger is saying something sassy to Fred. But even I can tell that she's flirting. "Now *that's* chemistry!" says Mom with a sigh.

Ginger lowers her eyelids to half-mast. Fred sings at her in a high, quivery voice. "Sounds like her chemistry turned him into a soprano," I say.

She punches my arm. "What do you know about chemistry? You're too young." Then she roughs my hair. "Thanks for cheering me up, Sunshine Boy."

I haven't been called Sunshine Boy since I was about five. I don't know whether to be embarrassed by the dumb name or glad she's feeling better.

Luckily the phone rings. I rush to the kitchen—maybe it's Dad. "Hello?"

"Hey, Jus." It's my used-to-be best friend, Ben. "You want to go to the mall with Cass, Jemmie, and me, take in the new *Lord of the Rings* movie? Clay says the battle scenes are awesome."

"How soon?" I ask, walking over to check the chicken.

"We have to make the five-fifteen because of school tomorrow. And we want to go early so we can hang out at the mall a while."

"That means leaving, like, right now." In the living room Mom is picking at a seam in the couch's upholstery. I can't leave her alone picking at the couch. "Sorry, I better stay here."

"I'm *begging* you, man. Cass and I can't go alone—her Dad doesn't let her date—and Jemmie hates being a third wheel. She won't go if you don't."

"Jemmie wants me to go?" I switch ears. "Me, specifically?" I lower the flame under the chicken a little—I could make the soup when I get back.

"She said you'd be okay."

I turn the flame up again. "Invite Leroy. He has the hots for her."

"She won't go if it's Leroy, only if it's you."

I turn the flame back down.

"Justin?" Mom calls. "Who is that?" Her voice sounds thin.

"It's Ben, Mom. Mind if I go to the mall?"

She hesitates. "All right."

"I'm in," I tell Ben. He says they'll pick me up in ten minutes. I stuff the change from the grocery store in my pocket and flop back down on the sofa. "We'll finish making the soup when I get home, okay?"

When Mr. Floyd taps the horn I give Mom a big kiss on the cheek—and I'm out of there.

○

I close the door behind me and take a deep breath of fresh, cool air, then sprint toward the flash of pink at the end of the path; the Pimpmobile awaits. I figure I'll dive in back, but the driver's window opens and Mr. Floyd hangs an arm out. "Want to ride shotgun?"

I trot around to the other side and fall into the deep leather front seat—the P-mobile has a nice interior. I say, "Hey," to Ben, Cass, and Jemmie, who share the backseat.

"Hey," Ben answers. He and Cass sit jammed together, leaving Jemmie most of the seat, but she's pressed against the door, as far from them as she can get. I'm looking past them back toward the house when Ben says, "Hey, Jus, find us some tunes. I don't trust Dad." Like my father, Mr. Floyd listens to country—music so bad it makes your teeth hurt. I get busy messing with the radio.

In front of the multiplex, Mr. Floyd taps his watch. "It's four-fifteen now. I'll pick you up at eight-thirty, right here. Got that, Ben?"

"Yeah, Dad, I got it."

We all climb out and the P-mobile pulls away.

We have an hour to kill before the movie starts. Jemmie and I tag along behind Ben and Cass, who are holding hands. We try to find things to do with ours. I stuff mine in my pockets. Jemmie hugs herself.

We've only been trailing them for a little while when she grabs the back of my shirt and jerks me into the door of the pet store. "Come on, Big, let's look around." Before going inside, she glares one last time at Ben and Cass, who keep on walking. "How long you think it'll be before they know we're missing? A week and a half?" She stalks into the store.

"Here we have your starter pets," I say. "Hamsters, gerbils, mice, rabbits, plus their way-cooler cousins, ferrets."

Jemmie asks the clerk if she can hold a white ferret. As soon as he hands it to her it goes up her sweatshirt sleeve. She gives a little shriek when its head pops out the neck of her sweat. I lift it off her shoulder. The ferret quivers like a small motor in my hands. Jemmie wrinkles her nose. "This animal stinks out loud." It's back in the cage for Whitey.

Next on the tour is the wall of dog tanks. Pups behind glass sprawl and sleep and gnaw rubber bones. Jemmie picks out a cocker spaniel with curly hair. "Isn't she sweet?" She pats the part of the glass the puppy is leaning against. "I'd name her Willow. How about you, Big? Which dog do you want?"

I choose a retriever. "I'd name him Stud."

"Stud!" she snorts.

"Spud," I say quickly. "Spud with a *p*. Let's check out the fish tanks." The back of the shop is dark, lit only by light bouncing off fish.

Jemmie brings her face so close to the tank of neon tetras, she breathes a white cloud onto the glass. "So pretty!" she says, wiping it with her sleeve. To me the fish that dart back and forth look like targets in a video game. I pretend to take aim and shoot. "What are you doing?" she asks.

"Nothing." My face gets hot. "Hey, look—goldfish." Goldfish aren't huge entertainment, but I have to get away from my dumb move at the neon tank. "I have this really big goldfish named Xena," I blab on. "She was tiny when I got her—she only cost ten cents because she was supposed to be food for other fish. Now she's big as this five-dollar fish, at least."

"Aw…" Jemmie hangs an arm around my neck. "She was supposed to be food, but you rescued her!" My face heats up again. "You must be her hero."

"Nah. To Xena I'm just the Giant Hand, deliverer of fishy flakes."

She laughs and gives me a little shove.

"Want to see some *really* cool fish?" I grab the sleeve of her sweatshirt and lead her over to a fifty-gallon tank. "Cichlids. They come from Africa and South America." A big cichlid with blue scribbles on its sides cruises up. Fanning the glass with a fin, it stares me down with one cold eye; it looks right through me. When it comes to pouring themselves into the Big Nothing, cichlids outdo even Mom.

Jemmie lets out a bored sigh. "That is the slowest, most do-nothing fish I've ever seen," she says. "Let's check out the snakes."

But the snakes are either buried in bark chips or coiled on

their electric hot-rocks. Jemmie thrusts out her lower lip. "Ectotherms are *so* boring." I know the word means cold-blooded; we're in the same science class.

I'm feeling pretty ectothermic myself, ready to curl up in a plush theater seat. But Jemmie, who is endotherm all the way, suddenly lights out for the door. "I'm hungry, Big. Let's hit the food court."

We order seven-layer burritos. I try to pay for hers too. "We're not on a date, Big."

"Definitely not on a date," I echo. When I do the math I'm glad she turned me down. Two burritos would have left me short for the movie ticket.

We're eating our dinner at a little round table under a fake tree covered with fake white flowers when Ben and Cass wander by. Oblivious, they're laughing and swinging their linked hands like five year olds.

"Gross!" says Jemmie. "Come on, Big Rig, let's go to the movies." She dumps ninety percent of a perfectly good burrito in the trash.

They don't allow outside food in the movies, so I decide I'll wrap mine in napkins and smuggle it in under my shirt. But when I pick it up it drools down my arm. A burrito under the shirt may not be the best idea. I cram a last big bite in my mouth and dump the rest. "You want to catch up with them?" I ask, my mouth full.

"Let them find us." She points a finger at me. "That is really gross. You should swallow before you talk."

We each buy our own ticket. As soon as we're in the theater Jemmie steers me into a seat: first row, dead center. "Best seats in the house, Big!"

We stretch our legs out. "This is where Ben and I always sit," I tell her.

"Cass likes the middle." She makes a face. "If I was with her I'd be back there with the old ladies." She turns to look, and sure enough, Ben and Cass are sliding into the granny section. Cass tries to wave us back to sit with them. I signal Ben to come on up. Nobody moves.

They sure miss a lot. Seated front row, center, we are practically trampled by Saruman's evil orcs.

If it had been me and Ben, we would've talked and made multiple raids on the snack bar. Jemmie lets me disappear into the story. I don't think about Mom, Dad, or Duane even once during the three-and-a-half-hour flick. Jemmie either, except for a second when her arm brushes mine.

○

I'm still thinking about the movie when I let myself back in the house, but I don't think about it for long. Smoke is billowing out of the kitchen. "Mom!" I race through the smoke, waving my arms. Mr. Chicken isn't doing the float anymore. All the water's gone. I burn my hand sliding the pot over to an unlit burner. "Mom?" I shout as I kill the flame.

I dash up the stairs. "You okay, Mom?" I try the knob, listen. I rattle the locked door. "Come on, Mom, you're scaring me." I pound the wood with my fists. "Mom!"

I hear the bed creak. "I'm okay...I'm resting."

I take a deep breath to make my voice stop shaking. "Resting's good... You want to watch another movie?" She doesn't answer. "Okay," I say, acting like she did. "Great. Come down whenever you're ready. Fred and Ginger are waiting."

Back in the kitchen, I open the windows to let some of the smoke out. I really screwed up. I went to the movies and wrecked the chicken; Mom had a relapse. But when I go to scrape the bird into the trash, I see it isn't *that* bad. The bottom's black, but there's still a lot of good meat on the top; probably enough to make soup—if I knew how. I look up a phone number and dial.

"Hello?"

"Hey, it's you, Nana Grace. This is Justin Riggs." I twist the cord around my fist. "You take your church hat off yet?"

I hear a low laugh at the other end of the line. "What can I do for you, Justin Riggs? You want my granddaughter?"

"No, I want to talk to you. Do you by any chance know how to make chicken soup?"

"Chicken soup? Child, I been making chicken soup since the Lord parted water and dry land. I'll tell you how to do it."

Nana Grace's chicken soup calls for a pinch of this and a little of that and "about enough to fill the bowl of your palm" of something else. Any ingredient I don't have she dismisses. "Never mind, child, jes' do without."

By the time we hang up I have the idea that chicken soup was any old thing you happen to have around—as long as it includes a chicken. How hard could it be?

Then I try to make it.

I unstick the bird and airlift it out of the pot. Midflight it caves in and lands splat on the floor, sending Giz barreling for the living room. I'm left holding the drumsticks.

Using a couple of spatulas, I pick the bird up, rinse off the cat hairs, and begin making soup—it was only on the floor for a few seconds.

First you gotta get all the skin off, Nana Grace said. Since there's already a greasy spot on the floor I pile the peeled-off skin there for the Giz. "Dinner is served," I call to the cat.

Next, she said, *you gotta get the bones out. You feel around good, now. There are some itty bitty ones.* I squeeze the bones out and toss them at the garbage can.

As I scrub strings of blackened chicken off the bottom of the pot, I remember the weird, electric feeling I got when Jemmie's arm brushed mine. I must've been resting on my elbow and the arm was half-asleep or something.

I find another big pot and put the good meat in it, add water, and turn the burner on low. I get out carrots, celery, and onions. "What about these onions?" I ask Giz, who's hunkered over the greasy pile on the floor. "Do I leave the skins on or peel them off?"

I dial the Lewises' house again. It rings four times before Jemmie's mother picks up. "Hello?" She sounds irritated. That's when I notice it's after eleven. "Hello, hel-lo?" I hang up quick. Hope she doesn't have Caller ID.

I taste a hunk of papery onion skin. It's like chewing a grocery store bag. I peel it off.

At 1:30 in the morning the stuff in the pot tastes a lot like soup. It's been hours since my three bites of burrito, so I serve myself a bowl. "Soup's on, Mom." My voice sounds as important as a penny falling on the floor. She won't even notice.

But then, like in a ghost story, I hear the scuff of feet on the stairs.

A washed-out, disconnected Mom sits down across the table from me. She blinks as if she's just come out of a cave. Between the greasy paw prints where the Giz walked away from his skin feast, the onion peels on the counter, and the mound of dirty dishes in the sink, the kitchen is pretty tragic. Her nose crinkles. "Smells like smoke."

"Our chicken kind of caught on fire. There was some major smoke, but it's okay now. Look, I finished making the soup." I hold a big spoonful of it right under her nose. "Open wide."

"Oh my gosh! I didn't even smell smoke upstairs. The house could have burned down!"

"It wasn't like it was flaming or anything. C'mon, Mom. Try some of our soup."

She opens wide and in goes the soup. "S'good." She runs her fingers through her hair. "What meal is this, dinner? Breakfast?"

"It's din-fast," I say and I grab the last clean bowl off the shelf.

I count the number of times she dips her spoon in. Three. She gives the rest to the Giz. He's going to be one fat cat if she doesn't get undepressed soon. "So, did Fred and Ginger live happily ever after?" I ask, wondering how long a person can live on two bites of sandwich and three spoons of soup.

"I don't know. I stopped the movie when you left," she says, as if she hasn't watched it a hundred times before.

"Hey, let's watch the end now."

Fred and Ginger are spinning across a marble floor when Mom says, "Your father called while you were out."

I try to keep the excitement out of my voice, out of my mind too. "When's he coming home?"

Mom shrugs. Her eyes stay on Fred, who seems to float, never quite touching the ground.

To PFC Duane Anthony Riggs:

Update from the trenches: Dad called in at nineteen-hundred hours last night. Situation remains hostile. Mom reported to work but may circle back to retake bed.

Provisions restocked with help of Nutrition Nazi Mrs. Lewis. Private Justin Riggs prepared chicken soup in middle of night. No fatalities or projectile vomiting, but troops are running on too little sleep.

Alert: Pvt. Justin Riggs about to go face down on desk in second period English.

I scribble a *J* on the bottom of the note. I'm headed for the *u* when a shadow falls across the page. I fake a cough and cover the paper with my arm so if Mr. Butler sees anything, it's the fact that I'm writing—and that's what I'm supposed to be doing.

He waddles forward and hovers over Jemmie, who sits in front of me. She has him for English, plus weekly piano lessons—a double dose of Butler. She doesn't look up, but in the shadow of Mount Butler her pencil picks up speed.

Her interest in the *Romeo and Juliet* essay is completely bogus. *Star-crossed, my foot,* she mumbled when she got her assignment. *Problem is they're too wimpy to tell their folks the way it is.*

Butler nods at her scribbling, then glides on like the Goodyear blimp. I nudge Jemmie's chair with my foot. "Unfortunate choice of names," I whisper, "Butt-ler."

She jabs back with an elbow—but it's true. Walking away, Mr. Butler is ninety percent butt, especially if you're looking up at him.

He docks in the gap between his chair and the board. The sleeves of his tight jacket ride up as he slaps a rhythm on the chair back.

I reread my note to Duane and crush it into a ball. Bet I could hit the can by Butler's desk with it. But if he caught me, the teacher's code would compel him to read the note to the class. I cram it into the pocket of my jeans and try to concentrate on the assignment, but Butler the one-man band is putting on quite a show. I'm probably the only one who knows why he reaches for a pencil. He needs it to get a better sound out of that chair. *Tick-tick,* he tests it against the wood and smiles.

It isn't long before Butler's wailing on the back of the chair, *slap-ba-bam-tick. Boom, slappa-slappa-slappa, boom, tick-tick-tick.* Jenny Stanley glances up from her paper and rolls her eyes at Trina Boyd.

Embarrassed for the guy, I focus on the nearest non-Butler thing: the back of Jemmie's neck. At first her neck is neutral, just a shape and a color—I start to drift toward the Big Nothing. But after a few seconds the neutral shape is a neck. A *nice* neck with a gold chain resting against it.

What if she feels me staring at her neck?

She doesn't seem to—until a sound like the last gasp of a dying beluga alerts her. Then she whips around in her chair. "You okay, Big?"

I wave a hand like it's nothing. I cough. She goes back to work on her essay.

I try to breathe normally, but I feel like·I've been hit by a truck. One second Jemmie's neck is just a handy gateway to the Big Nothing, the next it's attached to the prettiest girl in the room, or the school—possibly on the entire planet.

This is not good.

Things are shaky enough without me getting stupid over Jemmie Lewis. I remember the electric feeling when her arm brushed mine. Maybe that was an early warning.

The bell rings; I throw *Romeo and Juliet* in my pack. "Another forty-five minutes of our lives down the tube," I tell Ben, who sits behind me.

"And we get to flush the next forty-five solving for *x*."

"You coming?" I ask him.

"Gotta wait for Cass." He doesn't seem to remember that before Christmas break we used to walk to third together.

Jemmie grabs my pack strap as I walk toward the door. "Wait up." She's just showing Cass she doesn't need her, but all the blood in my body rushes to my face.

It's hard to breathe—and she'll be in front of me in algebra too. What if she catches me staring at her neck?

O

"Mom?" I stand in the living room, my pack hanging off one shoulder. "You here, Mom?"

No answer. It could be good news—she stayed at work like she was supposed to. Or bad news—she's buried under the covers. I sling the pack over the back of the sofa and hear an indignant *meow.*

I reach over and give the cat's bony head a scratch. "Where's Mom, Giz? Work or home?" I drape the Giz over my neck and climb the stairs. "And what do we have behind door number one?" I ask, feeling the silence inside her room.

I try the knob, thinking it might be locked, but it turns. The door opens on an empty room. "Way to go, Mom, still at work!" Then I see the bed. Her side is all messed up, like she's been wrestling the blankets. Dad's is smooth. The spread is still tucked under his pillow.

He's always been gone a lot, but this time feels different. I wish I could talk to him, ask him when he's coming home. That might be all it would take, but Mom claims she doesn't have a number or an address.

With a cat assistant it takes longer, but I manage to get the bed all nice and smoothed out—then I wreck it by smashing a fist into Dad's pillow. "Why aren't you home?" I land a couple more punches. "You're supposed to be home!"

I plunge down the stairs, hoping this will be the time, but there's still no car straddling the grease spot on the driveway. I press my forehead against the glass, lightly at first, then harder and harder. Experiment: How hard does a head have to push glass before it shatters? Head plus pressure applied to glass equals…???

Then I think of Mom—and ease off. I owe it to her to not put my head through a pane of glass.

Taking the stairs two at a time, I dig the cuff link out of my pocket. "You had your chance, and you blew it." I go straight to Dad's dresser and jerk a drawer open, intending to toss the cuff link in with his socks and boxers. The empty drawer clatters. I open another, and another.

All his drawers are empty. Does this mean that Dad doesn't live here anymore? I feel like such a jerk for not knowing. Then I think, it couldn't be that final.

I set the cuff link on the dresser and lean on my arms, panting. I stare at my parents' wedding picture. Dad holds Mom in his arms, all set to carry her into their first apartment. They look so happy. "Dad?" I say to the grinning guy with the full head of hair. "This isn't funny anymore. Get your butt home."

I walk away, then turn back and sweep the cuff link into my hand. I stuff it back in my pocket.

I jog down the stairs. Since I last checked, Dad's Town Car could have pulled into the driveway—along with the Starship Enterprise. I wouldn't see either one. I'm ignoring the view out the window. I retrieve my pack and check the fridge. I feel incredibly mad at Mrs. Lewis and her crappy, healthy food. I take an apple I probably won't eat upstairs and collect the Giz from Mom's bed. We retreat to Duane's room.

I close the door and take a quick sniff—I don't want to breathe all the smell out of the room, but I have to check to be sure it still smells like him. And it does. It's a mix of neat's-foot oil from his baseball glove and Tinactin: jock perfume.

Everything in the room is just the way it was when Duane left. The shelves are still crammed with baseball trophies and pictures of him and his old girlfriend, Lisi Bendix. I might flip through the stash of *Playboy*s in his bottom desk drawer once in a while—I even know about the two twenties hidden under them—but I always put everything back in the same order. I don't use his cologne or wear his clothes. Even the sock under the bed, all fuzzed-out with Giz hair, is exactly where he left it.

All I've done is add a couple of things. The plastic recorder on the nightstand is mine. My old Boy Scout sleeping bag is unrolled on the bed. It keeps the spread from getting dirty. I put Giz down on the bed. He walks over and curls up on the soft flannel. I lift him off to one side and flop down. I reach for the recorder. For maybe half an hour I make up this snake-charming kind of song. The notes flutter and slide. I get some amazing sounds out of that plastic tube.

I could keep on playing, but it's time to attempt the essay I didn't get around to in Butler's class. I hang over the side of the bed and slide the notebook out of my pack.

I'm supposed to explain the meaning of Mercutio's line "A plague on both your houses!" I think it means that in a fight that never ends, nobody wins, and everyone gets hurt. I just need to fluff it up so it fills at least a page.

I'm still fluffing when Mom comes in from work. "Justin?"

"Up here, Mom." At the sound of her voice I'm off the bed, ready to be her pal. I try a quick chin-up on the bar in Duane's door—which takes half a second since I can't do one—then I park one butt cheek on the banister and slide down. "Hey, Mom!"

But when I see her smeared eye makeup, my smile sets up like plaster of paris. "You have a good day?" I ask like always—a dumb question considering she's been crying.

"Fine," she says. "How was yours?"

"Fine." I wish we would tell the truth. *How was your day, Mom? Lousy. And how was yours, Justin? Triple lousy.*

She hugs a bucket of Kentucky Fried.

"You got supper. Great." I take the bucket out of her arms and hold out my free hand. "Let go." The bag of biscuits tucked under her elbow drops. "Now, put on something comfortable, I'll set the table." As she kicks off her heels I remember Dad muttering once, *I don't know why your mother wears high heels. They make her look like an elephant balanced on golf tees.* I laughed—it was pretty funny. But I wasn't laughing at Mom, I was laughing about the elephant.

As she drags up the stairs I notice a run in her left stocking and a stain on the elbow of her blouse. Were they there when she went to work? I gotta check her better before she leaves the house.

By the time she comes down in sweatpants and an old shirt, I have the table set as nice as the one at the Lewises'—candles and everything. I'm torching the wick of the first candle with one of Dad's throwaway lighters when out of the blue she says, "Oh, Justin... You haven't started smoking, have you?"

"What? No, Mom. I found this in the drawer."

"Your father started smoking at your age."

"Don't worry, Mom. I don't smoke."

"You know it can cause heart attack, emphysema, lung cancer...."

"Yeah, and it can also stunt your growth."

45

Mom gives it a rest. She knows I don't want to stunt my growth. "Well," she says, her shoulders relaxing a little. "Isn't this nice?" Then, instead of picking up her plastic fork and digging in, she folds her hands in her lap.

Maybe it's the folded hands, maybe it's the fact that she is so not-eating that I'm getting scared—but I insist that we say grace. If there's a God out there, and if He's actually interested, now might be a good time to get His attention; we could use a little help.

O

The phone rings right after dinner. "Hey, Jus." It's Duane. Nice to know there are some things I can count on, even without God pulling strings. "What's up, bud?" he asks.

"Did you get my emergency letter?"

"The one about the sneakers you need? I think there's some money in my room in the bottom desk drawer under some…uh…interesting magazines."

He means the forty dollars, but I can't spend it. It's part of the Duane archives. "I'm not talking about that letter, I mean the one about Dad splitting." Then I remember my fight with the hedge only happened yesterday. "Yeah, well, maybe you didn't get it yet. Dad blew out of here last Tuesday night. He hasn't been back." I keep my voice down, wanting to talk to him before Mom, who is in the next room watching *Wheel of Fortune*, figures out that it's him. "They had this huge fight."

"That's what they do, bro. It'll be all right."

"But he took everything, man. His drawers are empty."

That stops him for a second. "He's just taking the fight to a higher level. He'll come back. He always does. "

"Duane…"

"Right here, Jus."

"Has Dad ever cheated?"

"Cheated who?"

"Cheated on Mom!" I say in my loudest whisper. "I mean, if he messed around you would've told me, right?"

"Hey, Mike," he calls, covering the phone. "Can I bum a smoke?" Then he's back. "Listen, Jus. Have you and Mom been keeping up with the news?"

"No. We've been watching Pat and Vanna sell vowels. We *never* watch the news, you know that. Listen, about Dad—"

"You might start watching," he says, cutting me off. "Things are heating up in Iraq. The guys here think we're gonna get shipped over there soon as we finish training."

"What are you talking about?" I switch ears. "I thought you signed up to pump iron and learn something so you could get a decent job. You're a sports guy, not a fighter."

"That was before I joined the Army, bro. Besides, war is the biggest team sport in the world."

The headline in Mrs. Lewis's paper flashes in my brain: "President Ponders War." "You mean a real war? Like bullets and bombs and everything?"

Guess I forgot to keep my voice down, because suddenly Mom is right there, as animated as I've seen her since Dad's disappearance. She snatches the phone out of my hand. "Duane? What are you talking about?" She holds the receiver with both hands. "Duane, honey, are you all right?" When it comes to worrying about Duane, Mom goes from zero to a hundred in nothing flat.

Dear Duane,

Mom keeps saying she didn't raise her first son to get shot at. I guess that's what second sons are for. (Just kidding.) I can tell she wishes you never enlisted even if she won't say it. But I'll say it. For the record I wish you were still digging holes at FSU.

We quit watching real TV after you called. You know the closest we ever get to news around here is the weather channel, but as soon as we hung up we started surfing.

Ka-ching. We hit the mother lode—CNN. Did you know you can watch news 24-7? We pretty much do now. We eat in front of it. A couple nights we fell asleep there. As soon as she gets in from work Mom stakes out the couch. Most of the news has nothing to do with us, but we don't change channels. It's like we're waiting for the announcer to say, "And now for a special report on Private Duane Anthony Riggs."

I guess Dad knows about Iraq—he reads the paper and stuff. If he's worried about you maybe he'll come home. The family has to stick together, right?

Jus

P.S. Academic question: did you ever have trouble breathing around a girl? Not because she smells bad or anything, but just because— well—you know.

I reread what I wrote and it looks like I mean I *want* Duane in danger so Dad will come home. I don't, I silently tell whatever cosmic force might be listening.

I really, really don't.

I fold the letter into an airplane and launch it across the room. It crashes into the list of Acne Do's and Don'ts Mom tacked up on my bulletin board, then drops behind the desk. I crawl under and get it, then stuff it in an envelope, still folded.

The clock by my bed says six forty-three. Me, awake at six forty-three on a Saturday? This is unprecedented. It's still kind of dark out.

I listen for the drone of the TV from the living room—Mom was watching when I went to bed—but if it's still on, she must have the sound turned down low. I should have made her go to bed when I did. It's a little late now, but if she crashed on the couch I'll walk her up the stairs to her bed.

The house feels cold. I put on jeans, T-shirt, and sneakers. For a minute, I slide into the-room-that-time-forgot—the only place where everything is the way it's supposed to be—the Duane Riggs Memorial Bedroom.

I pick up one of the framed photos on the dresser. It's a shot of Duane in front of Leon High, holding up his baseball MVP trophy. "What am I supposed to do to cheer Mom up?" I ask him. The sucker doesn't answer. He just keeps on grinning.

Maybe I'll close the door and stretch out on the sleeping

bag; I could fall asleep again, easy. I set pitcher Duane Riggs back on the dresser, but his eyes stay on me. "I get ya, bro," I say. "Time to check Mom." But instead of checking, I reach for the recorder by the bed. As I play a short tune I look around. *All* the pictures of Duane are watching me. "Okay, okay." I toss the recorder on the bed. I try a dead hang pull-up on the way out; my elbows barely bend. *"Okay,* I'm checking!"

Creeping down the hall, I pass her closed door. Maybe she's in there—probably not.

But when I get downstairs, the only one in the living room is the cat, curled up in Dad's recliner. "Giz?" He doesn't twitch. "This isn't funny, Giz. Quit acting dead." I poke him in the ribs, half-afraid he'll be cold and stiff.

One eye opens. The Giz gives me a super-ticked-off look. I spoon some wet food into his bowl to thank him for not being dead—and then I split. I'll come back later and pull a Sunshine Boy, but Mom doesn't need me right now.

It's just getting light as I circle the neighborhood—as usual, I don't have anyplace to go. Wish I'd grabbed a sweatshirt— it's cold out. I dig my hands into my pockets, and there's Dad's cuff link. I pull it out and flip it as I walk. If I drop it I'll leave it where it falls, but I catch it every time. After a while I stick it back in my pocket.

Walking past Ben's, I hear a faint *tap a-tap a-tap* from behind the house; must be his dad, messing with one of the junkers. I wish I could stop in and see Ben, but unless he's going fishing with his dad or stocking shelves at the USA store, he doesn't roll out of bed until noon most Saturdays.

The first time around, I avoid Jemmie's street. I've tried all week to shake the idea that she's the prettiest girl in the world, but it's only gotten worse.

I never paid attention to how many classes we were in

together until my opinion of her morphed. Since then, from moment to moment, I always know right where she is. It's as if I'm wearing a pair of those heat-sensing goggles the Army issues to night fighters: wherever she is seems warmer than the rest of the room.

I pass her corner a second time, then think, hey, this is my neighborhood too. I walk back and turn on Magnolia Way. I do a little surveillance as I approach Cass and Jemmie's houses—they live next door to each other. Cass's house is like the others in the neighborhood, kind of small. Most of them were built by the Army in, like, 1950. But Jemmie's house is way older, and it's big. It was really fancy once, but it needs work. They've been painting it a little at a time ever since they moved in.

I glance at the lace curtains in one of the Lewises' upstairs windows and my heart skips a beat. That's her room. I forget who pointed it out to me, but I've known for a while—it just never mattered before. Now I can't take my eyes off the window. Jemmie is in bed in the room behind that curtain.

I wonder what a girl like Jemmie Lewis wears to bed. A baggy T-shirt, flannel pj's? Or is Jemmie the Victoria's Secret type? I hear a voice in my head—I swear it's Duane's—say, *Maybe she sleeps in the natural.* My ears are scorching when I hear a real voice. "Justin Riggs. My, aren't you the early bird?"

I've been so busy imagining what Jemmie's wearing (or not) I completely overlooked her grandmother, who's standing in the yard leaning on a shovel.

"Good morning, Nana Grace." I walk over to her, all nonchalant. "What are you doing?" I ask, hoping she doesn't notice my red ears.

She pushes up the sleeves of her sweater. "I'm diggin' a hole for my new tree."

The new tree is a bare stick poking out of a burlap sack. "I hate to say this, but I think it's dead."

"It just looks that way," she says. "Come spring, it'll put out a fine mess of new leaves." She hands me the shovel. "You remember how?"

"It'll come back." Last summer the two of us were part of a rescue mission to save trees from some woods that were about to be bulldozed. Somehow I ended up as Nana Grace's shovel man. We went around knocking on doors, seeing who wanted a tree. If a person showed the slightest interest, Nana Grace would sweeten the deal. *My boy here'll be happy to plant it for you. Happy to.* It was really hot that day. Still, I kind of liked going around with her.

"You're just the help I needed," she says as I step on the shovel. And suddenly it feels good to be digging a hole. I make it deep and wide and we stand the stick up in it. While she holds the stick straight I push the dirt back into the hole.

"Come on inside," she says when we've finished planting the tree. "I'll fix us a cup of hot chocolate." She's opening the door when I remember Jemmie and her pj's. Maybe she won't know I'm here...maybe she'll come down...and maybe—it won't be my fault if it happens—maybe I'll get to see her in them.

Things are working out perfectly—almost as if I had a plan—until Nana catches me darting my eyes up the stairs. "Oh, she's not here. She spent the night at Cass's."

That means no Jemmie slinking down the stairs in her Vicky's Secret lingerie—but it also means I might get to hang with Ben later.

Nana Grace opens a cupboard. "You're tall, can you reach that chocolate down?" No one's ever called me tall before—I guess tall is relative.

"When Duane joined the Army, Dad and I started drinking together—chocolate milk, I mean," I say, handing her the box. "We make it the barbarian way—no spoons. Just dump a pile of Quik in the milk and slosh it around."

"Don't it come out all lumpy?"

"That's the way we like it. The lumps are wet on the outside, dry on the inside; they bust open in your mouth..." I can't believe I'm going on about chocolate milk.

"Crunchy, huh? Guess every family's got their own ways. It's what makes family family. Now I hope you don't mind," she says, giving me a sideways glance and a grin, "but the way my mama taught me, you *gotta* stir the lumps out."

"Then I guess you gotta. Family is family."

"Ain't *that* the truth!" she says, shaking her head. "Family is family, no matter what." She pats my shoulder like she knows exactly what's going on at my house. Just because she doesn't talk about it doesn't mean she doesn't know. Nana's a person who can let things rest. The spoon scrapes the bottom of the pan as she stirs. Around and around. I hear a tune that goes with it inside my head.

As we sip our hot chocolate at the kitchen table, she watches me from under eyelids as wrinkled as a tortoise's. "Now, put that cup in the sink," she says when we finish. "It's time for your first piano lesson."

I walk my cup over to the sink. "Won't we wake up Artie and Jemmie's mom?"

"Them two could sleep through the Second Coming."

"Okay." I'm game if she is. Jemmie is out of the house, and I want to try it. "Get ready to cover your ears."

We sit side by side on the bench. As the folding lid hits the frame, the sound reverberates deep inside the piano. "Justin," says Nana Grace, "meet Mr. Sohmer."

"Who's Mr. Sohmer?" I'm about to look over my shoulder when I spot the piano maker's name neatly printed in gold across the inside of the lid: Sohmer & Co.

I run my fingers along the keys, feeling the flutter of the little breaks between them. The ivories are yellowed. Some of them are missing. Just the wood and the dingy remnants of old glue remain. Those keys feel rough, not smooth and satiny like the others. I jam my hands under my thighs. I must look really dumb feeling the keys. "What do I do?"

"You kind of noodle around. That's what I do. I just play how I feel. Most times it's some old hymn wants to come out my fingers, other times it's the blues. Sometimes what I play ain't got no name; I just make it up as I go along." She plays a snatch of melody, then leans toward me until her shoulder touches mine. "You know, playin' ain't as hard as folks make out. The music's all in here." She raps on the piano lid with a knuckle. "And in here." She does the same to my chest. "All you gotta do is let it out. Don't take much once you get started. Here's the general recipe."

First she shows me how to find a C. There are seven of them on the piano.

"You play in the key of C and it's simple. White notes all the way." Starting with what she calls middle C, she walks her fingers up to the next C: eight white keys. When she hits the fifth one nothing happens. "You gotta be patient with Mr. Sohmer," she says. "He's got two dead keys, a coupla slow ones too." She plays the run again, this time humming the missing note. "From C to shinin' C," she says. "That's a C scale."

She plays the same scale with her left hand, one C lower. Then both hands together.

Eight notes, five fingers. I watch closely to see when she crosses her fingers over so she can reach all eight keys—it's different for each hand. "Now you try," she says.

I play with my right hand first, hearing the silent G inside my head. Then I play the left, then both together, s-l-o-w-l-y.

She nods once. "Can't go wrong with C. It's a good, all-around key. With C you hardly ever have to mess with Mr. In-Between." She pecks at a black key. "Now this is how I mostly do. I play the melody with my right and chord with the left." She spreads the fingers of her left hand and strikes three notes at once. The sound stops as soon as she lifts her fingers. "Oh, yeah. If you want the sound to stick around, you gotta pedal."

We poke our heads under the piano to watch her push down a pedal with the toe of her sneaker. This time when she strikes the chord the sound rolls on and on. I feel my heart get bigger in my chest. Under the keyboard my fingers mimic hers, playing a silent chord on the knees of my jeans. "I want to try it," I say. "Can I?"

"Just do like I do. I'll play up here on the high notes, you play the low ones. Now find yourself a C down your end."

I find a C and spread my hand so that I can hit every other key using my pinkie, middle finger, and thumb. Kind of scared, I depress the keys so slowly all they do is click.

"Go on," Nana encourages. "Put a little muscle in it."

I strike the keys hard and the chord jumps out—I practically fall off the bench. "Sorry."

"Play loud as you want," says Nana, laughing. "Like the Good Book says, make a joyful noise."

I strike the chord harder, and she treads the pedal. The sound swells until it fills the house, all the way up to the room with lace curtains at the top of the stairs. I worry again about waking people up. "I bet Jemmie's mom thinks it's the Second Coming," I joke.

Nana Grace shakes her head. "We ain't bein' half as loud.

Besides, there'd be trumpets. Now keep your hand in the chord position and try shifting it up and down the keyboard."

By moving my hand I can play a whole slew of chords. And I don't have to hit the three notes at once; I can play them one after the other so they add up to a chord.

I feel Nana Grace's hand on my shoulder. "Sounds like you got a good ear, Justin." She gives my shoulder a squeeze, then pushes herself to her feet. "Mess around a while; I got stuff to do in the kitchen."

I slide to the center of the bench. Mine! All mine! The pedal and all seven of Mr. Sohmer's Cs are mine! I play a C scale softly, humming the dead G. Then I play a chord with my left hand. As I hold the pedal down the notes quiver. They still hang in the air when I begin to pick out a melody with my right hand.

Within minutes my left hand is booming out three-note chords, and I'm not even looking. But not looking, I accidentally let my middle finger hit a black key. The chord goes dark and sad.

"You stay away from them black keys!" Nana warns from the kitchen. "If you're feelin' down you don't need to be foolin' around with no minor chords."

How does she know I'm down? Come to think of it, how does she know half the things she knows? But as I shift my finger back to the white key, I realize that I'm not down. I'm not even worried. I've forgotten about Mom, and Dad, and Duane. I could sit here all day.

But now I *have* thought about Mom, who is home alone, probably awake now and sitting there by herself. I should go. I play a few more chords, slowly.

"Somethin' tells me you got more touch for music than you got for basketball," Nana Grace calls from the kitchen. "Ask your folks can they pick you up an old piano. They got 'em at the Goodwill sometimes; usually cost 'round a hundred bucks."

"I could ask... Listen, I better get home. I didn't leave my mom a note." I feel like I'm cutting Mr. Sohmer off right in the middle of the conversation when I close up the piano. "Thanks for the lesson."

"You're welcome to play anytime." She comes out of the kitchen, drying her hands on a towel. She squints, as if trying to bring me into sharper focus. "You know, Jemmie says she and Cass'll be staying after school on Mondays, Wednesdays, and Fridays to run. Track practice starts soon and they're gettin' ready. Stop by then if you want."

"Thanks. I'll try."

I hit the chill air as I jump off the Lewises' porch and run. I'm flying because I want to get home and check on Mom, but mostly I'm flying because I feel good.

O

Mom is at the sink doing dishes, whistling. I stand behind her for a second and just listen. I'd forgotten what a great whistler Mom is; I haven't heard her for a long time.

I walk to the table and add a drumroll. Mom turns. "There you are!" Her eyes are puffy, but she's smiling. "Where were you, Ben's?"

"Nowhere. Just walking around. How are you, Mom, are you okay?"

Her eyes look shiny like she's storing up tears, but she blinks fast and keeps smiling. "I've decided to be okay. I'm determined."

"Way to go, Mom!" I pick up the tune she's been whistling,

grab her by a soapy hand, and waltz her around the kitchen. In a second she's whistling too—harmony.

Mom giggles as I deliver her back to the sink with a graceful glide. "Thank you, Fred."

"You're welcome, Ginger."

"Margaret called," she says, and she pats her hair. "We're going to do a little shopping and then have lunch. Would you like to come?"

"Go out with the femmes? No, thanks. But you go ahead. Eat, see a movie. Have a great time." Margaret is the other secretary in the financial aid office. Margaret and Mom spend every day together, so what do they have left to talk about? Who knows? Who cares? The important thing is that Mom is leaving the house voluntarily.

When she walks out the door, I'm off duty. I grab the skateboard and head for Ben's—someone has to get that slacker out of bed.

○

"What do you think?" says Ben's mom, holding out the sides of her flowing tie-dyed skirt. "I dyed it myself."

"Nice."

"Thank God for weekends!" she says. "They give me a chance to get realigned with the universe."

"Yeah. The universe and I don't line up all that often either." I shift my weight. I really like Mrs. Floyd, but sometimes I don't know what she's talking about. "Mind if I wake up Ben?"

She drops the sides of her skirt. "You just missed him. He and Leroy left ten minutes ago. I think they were going to the school to play basketball."

As the door closes I wonder why they didn't pick me up. They went right by my house.

I roll away from Ben's, not sure of where I'm going. I could go home and keep Giz company, fix—and eat—a whole box of fish sticks, play a few video games.

I pass my house and keep going.

I expect to hear the bounce of the ball and Leroy and Ben panting and trash-talking. At first I think they aren't there, then I hear the slap of a basketball being tossed from hand to hand. They're sitting on the other side of the pecan tree that grows next to the track. I step on the tail of the skateboard and pick it up. I cross the grass quietly.

"I don't know what's up with that girl." It's Leroy talking. "I mean, I know she likes me."

"Don't call her for a few days," Ben says.

"Can't hurt to call!" Leroy sounds all defensive.

"Trust me, it can. If you call every night Jemmie'll take it for granted."

Ben's had a girlfriend for less than a month, and already he's an expert.

They must be tossing the ball higher. It's a long time between catches. "Guess I could skip a couple days," Leroy says at last.

"Do it. Make her worry."

When it comes to Jemmie, they are so clueless. She's not even looking for a boyfriend. If anyone's going to get next to her, it's me. I'm the one who goes to the movies with her. I'm the one she invites over for breakfast. As long as I don't screw up and tell her that I like her, I'll keep flying under the radar.

I'm about to back away from the tree and go when Ben says, "Are we here to shoot hoops or talk?" And they bound out from behind the tree, Ben holding the ball. "Hey, Justin." I can tell he's surprised to see me.

"Thanks for picking me up."

"Yeah…well…" He looks down and his hair falls across his face. I trot over to him and swat the ball out of his hands. Amazed the steal worked, I break for the court. The guys are on me in a heartbeat.

As Leroy lunges, trying to snag the ball, the red stripes at the tops of his tube socks flash. "Nice high-waters!" Then I feel cheap for saying it. Leroy's growing so fast his mom can't afford to keep up. Most of his clothes come from a cousin who's older, but shorter.

I feel Leroy's fingers on my back. "Just play the game," he says.

I make quick turns, trying to get off a shot, but it isn't going to happen with Leroy guarding me. He's tall, really tall, and his arms are everywhere. It's a miracle I retain possession.

"Take your shot, Lard."

A flash of anger goes to my muscles. "You got it, jerk." Without thinking, I turn, jump, and shoot. Bad as I am at basketball, it should miss by a mile. Instead, it catches the rim and circles it. It's about to go down the drain when a long arm, sticking way out of the ragged end of a sweatshirt sleeve, slaps it away.

"Hey," I shout. "I been robbed!"

Leroy chases it down, then runs it in and dunks it. "Aw, poor baby." He hangs from the rim, his shirt hiked up. Wow. For a skinny guy he is really ripped.

Ben catches the ball and tosses it to me. I guess it's some kind of consolation prize for not coming by for me this morning. I throw it right back, a hard shot to the chest. "It's your ball." He stares at me for a split second, then turns and sinks it. After that it's every man for himself, and it gets brutal.

Time after time Leroy the octopus snags the ball before I can get a finger on it. Ben takes plenty of shots too. When it comes to the ball, Ben is psychic. He just seems to know where it's going. Since he's fast, he beats it there by half a step. He and Leroy cut in and out, dribbling with both hands. I dodge around and wave my arms. I'm only in the action when one of them runs into me.

I'm off to one side watching when Leroy rattles another one through the hoop. "Nothing but net!" he yells. There hasn't been a net as long as we've played here, just a rusty hoop, but Leroy has a hyperactive mouth.

Ben snags it on the rebound, drives to mid-court, turns, and launches a jumper.

The shot ricochets off the backboard—straight at me. I make a fingertip catch, expecting it to get away, but I hold on. With Leroy bearing down on me I take a wild shot, knowing I'll miss. It goes through and bounces right back into my hands. My second shot scores too.

From then on I'm golden. I can't miss. Justin Riggs and the universe have aligned! The only thing that could make it more perfect would be Jemmie cheering on the sidelines: "Go, Big Rig! You rule!" But she's not here. Besides, Jemmie's never stayed on the sidelines in her life.

We shoot hoops until it hurts to breathe and we've sweated through our T-shirts. Leroy collapses against me, an arm over my shoulders. "I give up. Today you're the man, Big Rig."

I jerk away from him. "Why'd you call me Big Rig?"

"Why?" He pops me on the shoulder with his palm. "Because you're big. I mean, look at yourself."

I feel kind of sick. I thought Jemmie only used that name when it was her and me, but she must have called me that when she was talking with Leroy. He calls her every night.

"I just remembered something I have to do." I walk off the court and flip my skateboard over. "Catch you guys later."

Ben trots after me. "What do you have to do?"

"Just stuff." The three of us head back to the neighborhood.

When we get to Leroy's house, he falls out. "Later," he says. His mom cleans a real estate office on Saturday afternoons. Leroy and his brother go with her. Leroy mops the floors.

"Want to eat lunch at my place before you do your stuff?" Ben asks me.

"Yeah, okay."

His mom makes us cheese and bean sprout sandwiches, then we go out back and change the filters on one of the Vehicles of Promise. Ben's head is under the hood when I catch sight of Cass weaving between the cars like a cat. When she reaches us she puts her palms on the fender and lifts up on her toes, leaning toward Ben. "Hey."

He looks up and flicks his hair out of his eyes. His face lights up. "Hey yourself."

I hand Cass the wrench I've been holding for him. "See ya."

"Wait," says Ben. "Stick around, Jus." I don't look back as I walk away, I just hold up my hand, like, bye. I know when I'm extra.

I skate by Jemmie's on the off chance she'll see me. When I find her on the porch swing I act surprised. "Hey, Jemmie!" I drag a toe. With each forward swing she kicks off the porch rail as hard as she can. On the backswing she practically hits the window. "Want to ride?" She shrugs like she doesn't, but she jumps out of the swing. The chains are still clattering when she hops aboard.

We go real fast but the problem is the same as ever: nowhere to go. An old lady is wheeling her garbage can into the street and we almost knock her over. I yell, "Sorry, Mrs. Zelinsky!"

When we've circled the same block for the third time I head for the cemetery.

"Not much to do here but act respectful," says Jemmie, hopping off the board.

I fish the Superball out of my pocket. "Let me show you how to play 'Dead-Guy Baseball.'" I'm hoping my hot streak on the basketball court continues.

In less than ten minutes she's whipping my butt.

O

By the time I get home it's late afternoon. Mom's in her nightgown, collapsed on the sofa. "They're shipping another twenty thousand troops to the Gulf, Jus."

My heart jumps into my throat. "You hear from Duane, Mom? Is he going?"

"No, but just look…" On the tube, guys in desert fatigues hug their wives and mothers. "Any one of them could be Duane."

I step between her and the tube. "How was lunch with Margaret? What did you two eat?"

"Cuban sandwiches." She takes a swipe at my knees. "Move your little fanny so I can see what's going on."

I fall into Dad's recliner.

About eight, I fix each of us a bowl of Mrs. Lewis's healthy puffed wheat cereal: Mom's with milk and sugar, mine dry.

Mom takes one bite and makes a face. As she sets the bowl on the coffee table the spoon begins to slide. She does nothing. She just watches it disappear under the milk.

"Help me," I squeak. "I'm drowning!" She doesn't even crack a smile, so I shift into a deep, manly voice. "Thought you couldn't grow a mustache?" I say. "Well, now you can! In just seconds you can go from this—are you watching, Mom? From this…" I smile. "…to this!" I lick my upper lip quick and plunge my face into my bowl. I come up with wheat puffs stuck all over my lip, like a mustache of bees, and I finally get a laugh.

As my grin gets wider puffs start falling off. Mom laughs harder. She reaches over and gives my leg a squeeze. "You are my sunshine," she sings, "my only sunshine…"

"Thanks for the musical tribute," I say. But I feel kind of tired. It's hard work being someone's sunshine.

O

I wake up at three-thirty in Dad's recliner with a wicked crick in my neck. Mom's bowl, still on the coffee table, is dry, every drop of milk gone. The spoon is balanced across the inside of the bowl, spanning it like a bridge. A few soggy wheat puffs are all that's left of Mom's dinner. This has to be the work of the Giz.

"Mom?" I touch her shoulder. She whimpers in her sleep and pulls away. On the tube they're running a story about the frigid temperatures in Europe, and suddenly the house feels cold. I cover her with an afghan and go upstairs.

I walk into Duane's room, not mine. I wrap myself in the sleeping bag. But now I'm awake. I lie on my back looking up. Light from the street grazes the half-dozen model planes that form a shadowy squadron above the bed. Duane and Dad built them a long time ago. They told me I was too young to help.

Dear Duane,

You remember that old keyboard in your closet? I hope you don't mind but I'm using it. It doesn't play anyway. Not since Dad put his foot through the amp by "accident."

If you don't like me messing with it you can come here and beat me up. (Another slick plan to bring Private Riggs home.)

You're probably wondering why I'm screwing around with a dead keyboard. Jemmie's grandmother is teaching me to play the piano. With the keyboard I can work on my fingering—and no one will suffer. You know everyone suffered when you played—at least until Dad's little accident.

Speaking of Dad, it's been almost two weeks since he blew out of here. Should I start worrying?

Justin

P.S. I wish you could talk to him.

Nana Grace doesn't seem one bit surprised to see me at her door. She puts her hands on my shoulders and walks me right to the piano, steering me around Artie.

I step over his truck. "Hey, Artie."

"*Vrooooom*," says Artie.

"Make yourself at home," she says as she uncovers the keyboard. We sit down on the bench. She starts lesson two right where we left off. "C is the only key you play white notes all the way." She plunks out a C scale. "Any other key you gotta slide over to black here and there." She moves one white key up from middle C and pecks it with a stiff finger. "Start on D. See if you can feel it out."

And that's the whole lesson. She says she's in the middle of baking some cookies, but I think she knows I want to mess around by myself. She even picks up Artie and his truck. "Come on in the kitchen now and help Nana."

After that it's just me and Mr. Sohmer. We have a whole hour before Jemmie gets home. I lace my fingers together and flex them, then put my thumb on D.

It takes two black keys to make the D scale sound right. I run the scale up and down, up and down. One hand. Both hands. I don't even screw up when I have to change fingering to hit the notes at the top of the scale—practicing on Duane's keyboard is paying off.

After a while, the D scale becomes automatic. Playing it, I think about the tough day Mom and I put in yesterday. We watched *Casablanca* with Humphrey Bogart, one of her favorites, but not exactly what she needed. She cried when Bogart's character Rick tells Ilsa good-bye and puts her on the airplane. It reminded her of soldiers boarding planes and ships for the Persian Gulf. It reminded her of Dad. She slobbed up a bunch of tissues before I could distract her with *The Simpsons.*

But watching Bart and Homer bummed *me* out. Bart and Homer, father and son. The father and son team at our house was always Dad and Duane, not Dad and me. The scale I'm playing drags, like it doesn't have enough energy to climb from one D to the next.

I stand on the pedal and hammer the keys. I release the pedal for the next run up the scale and the notes snap off clean. *Jab-jab-jab,* like a rapper poking a finger at the camera, all in-your-face.

"I hear you, Marvin," says a voice just inches behind me. "This boy's got the touch." A napkin with a hot chocolate chip cookie on it plops down on top of the piano. I stop playing to ask about Marvin, but Nana puts a hand on my shoulder and leans forward. "You 'bout got D licked." She fingers the next key. "See what you can do with old man E," she says and then goes back to cookie central.

The E scale takes five blacks. Five! If this keeps up I'll be hitting nothing but black keys.

But F and G only have one each, which is encouraging. "I'm moving to the key of H," I yell toward the kitchen.

Nana Grace laughs. "Ain't no key of H. After G you go to A."

"A comes after G?" Weird. I'm glad I play by ear.

The A scale has three black keys, B has five, then it's back to good old C.

After rippling the scales up and down, I decide to make something up in C. I remember the sad sound I got when I threw in a black key, so I try it. What did Nana Grace call a chord like this? Oh, yeah, minor. I play the chord again. It reminds me of the way Mom looks these days—like she's on the edge of tears.

All I have to do to make the chord cheerful as "Happy Birthday to You" is slide my middle finger off the black key and onto the white again. Happy and sad are that close together.

I find a few chords with my left hand. When I have a sequence that works, I start stringing a tune along the top with my right. It's frustrating at first; I can hear the tune in my head clear as anything. After a while though, after I repeat it over and over, the piano begins to sing my song back to me.

I don't know how long I've been at it when a dark object traveling at the speed of light darts over my shoulder. When I turn, Jemmie is taking a big bite out of my cookie. "Didn't know you played, Big," she says with her mouth full.

"I don't." My hands turn to bricks and plunge into my lap.

"Sounds like you do." She flounces down on the piano bench beside me, so close I see that the little curls along the edge of her forehead are damp. She plays a chord, then pinches the neck of her T-shirt, pulls it out an inch, and takes a whiff. "Whew! Breathe through your mouth."

"You smell okay," I say. Actually, she smells sort of spicy. Is that what girls smell like when they sweat?

"No I don't." She crosses her eyes at me. "I stink."

"Try the guys' locker room sometime."

"Pa-leez." As quickly as she plopped herself down she jumps back up and tosses what's left of my cookie on the napkin. She shouts, "I'm taking a shower, Nana," and sprints up the stairs.

Her bite has turned my cookie into a grin. The edge is scalloped with the shapes of her teeth. I take a bite in the same place, just a little bigger than hers. This is really sad. I'm deliberately eating Jemmie's spit.

I fold the rest of the cookie up in the napkin and stuff it in my pocket. I'm about to close the piano when the shower starts running upstairs; Jemmie can't hear me now. I'll play my tune one more time.

One time flows into the next, and the next. It's hard to stop. I've played it half a dozen times before I finally close the lid and push the bench back. "Bye, Nana Grace. Thanks."

She comes out of the kitchen holding a pan of cookies with a pot holder. Artie follows her, a cookie in each hand. "You sure you don't wanna stick around 'til Jemmie comes down? Coupla these cookies got your name on 'em."

"No thanks. I need to get home."

"See you Wednesday then."

"Okay. Maybe."

Nana purses her lips. "Why, Justin Riggs," she scolds. "You got a talent, and God don't give out talent so it can sit in the dark like a seed beggin' for light."

Talent? Suddenly it's like I have something extra inside me, something smooth and heavy. "Jemmie'll be running Wednesday?"

"Every Monday, Wednesday, and Friday."

"I'll be here," I call after her as she and Artie go back into the kitchen.

I hear the soft, hurried tread of bare feet on the stairs.

"*Psssst...* Hey, Big!" Jemmie whispers. Her head is wrapped in a white towel. She squeezes the rail with both hands and leans out to me. I catch a whiff of vanilla. "Stick around, Big. *Please...* I don't want to practice piano!"

"Sorry, sweetheart. Gotta go."

What just happened? I wonder as I close the door behind me. *Sweetheart?* Who do I think I am? Humphrey Bogart? Jeez, I've been watching too many of Mom's old movies. Jemmie practically begs me to stay and I turn her down. *Then* I call her sweetheart and leave her with her mouth hanging open.

Actually, it's kind of cool.

○

The phone rings at eight. Duane time. "Got it, Mom!" I snatch up the extension in the kitchen. "Hey, Big Booger!"

"Hey, L'il Booger," says the friendly salesman's voice at the other end of the line. "How ya doin', son?"

I feel this weird surge of hope. "Hey, Dad! Where are you? You coming home? It's been two weeks."

"I'm still in Atlanta."

The miles loop out between us as I listen to the silence on his end of the line. "You at a motel?"

"Where else would I be?"

"I don't know, Dad, you tell me."

"Is that Duane?" Mom calls from the living room, over the sound of the TV.

"No, Mom." She turns back toward the set. She must assume it's Ben or somebody.

"So, how's it going, bud?"

I scrape at something stuck to the table with my thumbnail. "It's going okay."

"Really? You're really okay?"

"Mom and I are doing great."

There's a long pause. He clears his throat. "None of this is about you. You know that, don't you? We're still pals, right?"

"You're never around, Dad." I lean against the table and the cuff link in my pocket digs into my leg.

"Come on, I've always been gone a lot."

"Not like this you haven't. I don't even know how to get in touch with you. Can't you at least give me a number I can call?"

He sighs. "I'm not real settled now, but I'll call you every couple of days, how's that? Fair deal? Don't forget, I love ya, bud."

"Love you too," I mumble.

"All right! Now, can you put your mom on?"

"Yeah, I guess." I hold the phone and listen to his breathing on the other end of the line. Seems like I have something more to say to him, or he should have something more to say to me. I'm about to give up and get Mom when I hear a woman's voice. "You going to be much longer, hon?"

"Who was that?" I demand, my stomach feeling strange.

"It's the TV, Jus. I bumped the mute button accidentally." His voice is so relaxed it's got to be the truth. "Now would you get your mother? I need to talk to her about Duane."

I turn to yell for her, but Mom is already standing in the door. I hold the phone out. "Dad."

She takes it. "What do you want, Jack?" She sounds more tired than mad. "Yes, Duane says there's a chance he'll have to go. He told us that a week ago. You'd know if you called more often." She pauses. "I'm not being snide, Jack. I'm just stating the facts." She turns, twisting the cord around her body, and drops into a worried voice. She tells him the rumors Duane's heard.

She holds up a hand like she always does when she wants him to stop talking. "I know, Jack. I know he volunteered. But do you really think he's up to it? Remember the time he went

73

orienteering in Scouts? He got lost in three acres of woods."

That gets Dad started. I know he's telling the story when she says, "Longer than that, Jack. I swear he was in there two hours."

All kids have embarrassing stories about them that get told and retold—personally, I have dozens. Getting lost in three acres of woods is one of Duane's. When he finally stumbled out Duane went right up to the troop leader. He told Mr. Cooper it was his job to staple moss to the trees—how else was a scout supposed to figure out which way was north? That's the punch line. I can tell when Dad says it because Mom laughs.

Normally I would laugh too, but I feel off balance. I keep hearing the voice on the other end of the line: *You going to be much longer, hon?* The more times I play it over, the more I think, yeah, it was the TV, until I'm about ninety-nine percent sure.

Mom hangs up. "He'll call again tomorrow to hear what Duane has to report." She presses her fingertips against her lips and blinks fast. "Did he sound...lonely to you?"

I shrug and look away. Mom reads eyes. I don't want her to read mine and see the one percent that believes Dad had some woman in his room.

Mom's just settled on the couch when the phone rings again. I run to the kitchen and pick it up. "Hey," I say, but with less enthusiasm.

"Hey, Jus!" Duane says. "You sound down. What's the problem, man?"

"You first. Are you shipping out?"

"Yeah—looks like. We've been tying down tanks and Bradleys to ship over. I got my first anthrax shot. Nothing's official 'til I get my Permanent Change of Station next week, so don't get bent out of shape. And whatever you do, stay cool with Mom. "

I want to talk longer, but all of a sudden Mom is breathing on my neck. "Would you give me that phone?" I pass it to her. She peppers him with questions, but gets paler and paler listening to the answers. She's silent when she passes the phone back.

"Mom sounds a little shaky, Jus," he says. "Don't be running around with the guys all the time. Help her out, okay?"

"I *haven't* been running around with the guys. But what am I supposed to do?" I watch Mom drift up the stairs to her room. "She's worried about you, she's worried about Dad. She's a mess."

"I'm sorry you got stuck with all this, Jus. Don't worry about Dad though, he'll come home. And me, I'm safe for another week and a half, minimum, so don't sweat it. Let's talk about something normal. Tell me what's up with you."

I don't want to tell him about the possible woman in Dad's room—so I blab about Jemmie. "Listen, I have a question, no big deal, but do you think there is the remotest chance that Jemmie Lewis could ever be even slightly interested in me?"

"Interested like she thinks you're a nice guy, or interested like baby, oh baby?"

"The second one—only leave out the 'oh babies.' What do you think?"

He whistles between his teeth. "Tall order, Jus. How's the Clearasil battle going?"

"It's been pretty tense around here."

"Scrambled eggs, huh?"

"Not funny, Duane." My brother never had the problem. Kid Zitless doesn't know what it's like to be afraid to see his own face in the mirror. "You know, I'm not the worst-looking

75

guy in the world. She laughs at my jokes... So what do you say? Do you think I have a lottery chance?" A lottery chance is what my brother and I call it when the odds are, like, a bazillion to one.

"Yeah, well...I *guess* it could happen."

"Don't hurt yourself getting enthusiastic or anything."

"Listen, little bro, let me give you a few great girl-getting tips. Guys have paid big bucks for what I'm about to tell you. You might want to take notes."

"Just tell me." For a second I think he's going to say something that might actually work.

"Tip number one, don't act like you want it."

"Gross, Duane! I *don't* want it."

"Calm down. I'm not talking about the big 'it.' I mean, like, making out."

"Oh." I hold a finger to my head and pretend to pull the trigger. Why did I have to tell him about Jemmie?

"Tip number two," Duane continues, "ask her questions. Girls like to hear themselves talk."

"Guys have paid for this?"

"Shut up and listen, young Skywalker. Tip number three, never spill your guts. Girls act like they want you to spill. But trust me on this, you spill, and they think you're just another girl."

He gives me a few more—tell her she has pretty eyes, make friends with her pet—but he has to go because a bunch of other guys are jockeying to use the phone.

We hang up and I sit listening to the fluorescent bulb buzz overhead. Even my own brother doesn't think I have a one-in-a-bazillion chance. The universes of Jemmie Lewis and Justin Riggs are destined to spin right past each other, not collide.

I remember the scene at the beginning of *Casablanca*, when Rick and Ilsa catch sight of each other across Rick's Café

Américain. They haven't seen each other for a long time, but the look between them is like a match touching a sparkler.

I recast the movie in my head. Now it stars Jemmie and me, years from now. We see each other across Justin's Café Américain. My skin is clear. I'm six-two or six-three and cool as Bogart.

"Big...?" I can tell by the way she says it, that she means tall, not fat. "Big? Is that you?" She sounds a little breathless.

In my imagination I keep walking toward her, walking toward her, only when I get close, guess who's standing there?

Private Duane Anthony Riggs. How did *he* get in the middle of my remake of *Casablanca*?

A week and a half. He says he'll be safe for that long, at least. A week and a half? Big whoop. At our house, dishes sit in the sink longer than that.

Dear Duane,

Mom and I have been talking it over. The war's not a definite yet. The UN could still work things out. Maybe you won't even have to go. Mom's got everyone at work praying for you and some of them are real religious.

And now for the local news—my grades are taking a dive. They're not as bad as the scum-sucking grades you used to bring home—but they're bad. I can't focus Right now I'm in algebra. Instead of paying attention I'm writing to you. Pretty pitiful considering nine chances out of ten I won't even mail this.

You should hear me on the silent keyboard though! I sound even better on the Lewises' piano but when I can't go over there I take the keyboard out and mess around. Too bad they don't give grades for silent keyboard. I'd kick butt.

BTW, that stuff I said about me & Jemmie? It's no big deal. Forget about it.

Justin

The first clue I have that Jemmie is behind me is the zing of an icy Coke can on my back. I whip around on the piano bench, jerking my shirttail out of her hand. "Hey," I gasp. "Are you getting personal?"

She laughs. I can practically read the thought bubble over her head: Dream on, fool.

But as I leave her house I run the tape over and, I'm sorry, but sticking a Coke up someone's shirt is personal. I stop on their porch a moment to think about it and catch my reflection in their storm door.

Hey, am I getting taller? Looks like it.

Maybe Duane's full of crap. Maybe I *do* have a lottery chance.

I climb my front steps. I'd like another look at my possible growth spurt, but there's a rusty screen, no glass in the door. The replacement window, which is propped against the garage, is coated with dust. The screen should have been switched out months ago, but no one's done it.

I let myself in. "Hey, Giz, what do you say, am I getting taller?" Giz is asleep on the stack of unopened mail on the coffee table. He twitches a paw. An envelope sails to the floor. As I pick it up I see it's a bill from MasterCard. Dad always pays the bills. Mom hasn't done a thing about them since he left. She just flips through the mail, pulls out the magazines, and leaves the rest on the table. I hope MasterCard can wait.

I lift the cat to stuff the bill back, but under Giz is an

envelope from the utility company. The city turns your lights off if you don't pay. It's happened to some of our neighbors.

I rake all the mail out from under the cat. I come up with eight potential bills. Might as well check and see when they're due. The one from the utility company is due next Tuesday. Better alert Mom.

When I open the one from MasterCard I let out a whistle. "Eight hundred and thirty-two dollars!" I unfold the page and read the first charge: The China Pearl. Sounds like a restaurant. The Magnificent Table. Another restaurant. There are charges from four restaurants, each followed by a phone number and the letters GA. All these charges were run up in Georgia—Atlanta, maybe.

The tabs are big. The one from La Cucina is for ninety-seven bucks. Even Dad can't eat his way to a total like that. Maybe he's taking out clients. But would he take people who own restaurants to other restaurants? Or maybe these dinners aren't business. If that was a woman I heard in his room, she might be helping him run up the bill, spending our family's money.

I don't know, though. Most of the other charges look okay. There are a bunch from gas stations and a couple from a discount store. I stuff the bill back in the envelope. Giz lets out a complaining *meow* when I shove it and all the other bills back under him. "Not my department, Giz."

But it's like I've hidden a bomb under the cat. If I tell Mom about the utility bill she might check them all out. One look at MasterCard and she'll see candlelight dinners and Dad pouring wine for someone else.

I'm still staring at the cat when I hear three quick knocks on the front door followed by two slow: Ben's signal.

He's already heading toward the street when the sound of the opening door catches him. "Hey," he says, trotting back up the steps. The screen tints him copper like he's real tan. "How goes it?"

"It goes." As I nod my head I feel like it's not all the way attached to my neck. The old Ben would have noticed something was wrong. Not this one. He nods back. We hang like that for a second, him on the porch, me inside, both of us nodding like we've just exchanged the Great Secret of the Universe.

I should hold the door open for him—he's seen our place trashed before. When he was in and out all the time it was no big deal. These days he seems like company.

I go outside. We sit on the steps, elbows on knees, chins in our hands. "Why aren't you with Cass?" I ask.

"We had a fight." He lets out an exasperated sigh. "You understand girls, Jus?"

"Understand girls?" I think about Jemmie and the Coke can. "No way. They're inscrutable."

"Inscrutable," Ben agrees and we both go silent.

I think about showing him the bill, but don't. His dad would never do stuff like that. "Hey, Ben, help me put the storm window in the door, okay?" We both jump up, glad to have something to do besides search for lame things to talk about.

I'm all for installing the window as is, but Ben says we should get the dirt off first. He drags the hose around the side of the house; I get a sponge. I'm standing there holding the sponge when he turns toward me. Hose nozzle in hand, he takes aim about crotch level, grinning like the old Ben.

"Don't even think about it, Ben Floyd!"

As he squeezes the trigger, I lunge. We wrestle for the hose. Icy water geysers. I hook his ankle with a foot. *Bam*, we're rolling on the ground, water spraying everywhere.

We don't notice the girls until we hear them giggle. By then they're running away. We jump to our feet. Ben drops the hose and watches Cass sprint off, ponytail flicking side to side. I watch Jemmie.

My shirt clings to my chest. Jeez, do my nipples show? I pull my shirt out fast. "You ever wish things were the way they used to be before you got together with Cass?" I ask. "You know—normal."

He gazes down the street like he hopes she'll come back.

I grab him by the back of his wet shirt. "Come on, Romeo. Let's dry off." He follows me inside. The mess isn't *that* bad.

"Got to be a couple of towels in here somewhere," I say, digging through the mound of clean laundry Mom dumped on the sofa a couple of days ago. I mined it for pants this morning and found some crushed at the bottom of the pile. The wrinkles smoothed out some as the day went on.

Mom has started doing things around the house again. She doesn't finish, but at least she starts.

I find a couple of towels and we dry off. To clear the sofa we have to fold the laundry. Ben sticks to neutral things like sheets and T-shirts. I do Mom's stuff. There would be something creepy about having a buddy fold your Mom's clothes. Ben understands.

After folding laundry and watching MTV for a while, we go back to the window job.

We've just installed the window when Mom rolls into the driveway. I step aside, and gesture at the sparkling glass like Vanna White. Ben falls back a step and grins. No way she can miss it, but she does. The first words out of her mouth are "State of the Union tomorrow night."

"State of the what?"

"The president is giving the State of the Union address tomorrow night."

"And this is important because...?" I say, waiting for her to fill me in.

She hugs her purse to her chest. "He may say whether or not we're going to war."

Ben scuffs the porch floor with a sneaker. "It'll be a bad night at my house if he says we are. Dad has tons of old students in the Army, Marines, Navy. He encourages them to sign up so they'll get an education."

Mom's eyelids flutter as if she's waking up. "I know. He helped Duane make up his mind."

"Sorry. My mom always gets on him about that. She doesn't believe in violence, even if you get a free education."

"Mom," I interrupt. "Back it up a second? Could you at least notice the storm window? We installed it. Ta-dah!"

I know it's a really small thing compared to finding out if there's going to be a war, but for some reason it's important to me to get credit. I can't stop the war but I do what I can.

I watch Mom climb the steps in the wavery reflection on the window. "Thanks, you two," says the alternate Mom who is walking toward me from the wrong side of the glass. "It's the little things that make life seem normal, isn't it?"

Ben falls back a step. "Guess I'd better go." I can tell she's freaking him out. His own mother dresses like a hippie—burns incense and everything—but she's normal on the inside. My mother *looks* normal, but on the inside she's Bizarro Mom. Ben jumps from the top step to the ground.

"Wait up," I say, dropping onto the path beside him. "I'll walk you."

We set off for his house like we've done a million times. Before Cass, we would mess around at his place a while, then he'd walk me home. On a weekend we could go back and forth like that for two days. But I can tell Ben has other things on his mind.

"Think I'll call her," he says. "Or would that be too dumb?"

"Not as dumb as swimming with piranhas."

He gives my shoulder a quick jab with his fist.

"Okay, *okay*," I protest. "Call her, just don't sound pitiful. Don't beg or anything. Try to get *her* to apologize." I turn and walk backwards ahead of him. "Say Ben. Do you by any chance know how to write checks?"

"Checks?"

"Yeah, those paper things that act like money."

"Oh, sure. I have full access to my parents' account. I write checks for whatever I want."

"No, seriously. Do you know how to write one?"

"Leroy does. He pays the bills for his mom." He stops in front of his house. Hands in his pockets, he rolls his shoulders forward. "You really think it's okay if I call her?"

I hold my hands out and pretend to shake a Magic 8 ball. "The Great 8 says 'All signs point to yes.'"

He shrugs. "Okay, I guess I might." He fakes a turnaround jump shot and slaps the edge of the roof over the front door.

"Catch you later," I say.

Ben doesn't answer. The storm door shuts behind him with a snap. Bet he's dialing her number before I even reach the street.

O

I'm about to knock but I hesitate. I've never gone to Leroy's without Ben. Feels funny. I knock softly. The TV is on inside. When nothing happens I knock again, harder. Leroy opens the door partway. "Hey, Big Rig." He doesn't smile.

"Mind if I come in?" His expression stays the same, but he opens the door a little wider, pushing it with the tips of his long fingers. There are hardly any lights on in the living room.

I say hey to his brother Jahmal, who's parked in front of the TV. The kid doesn't answer. He has two little TVs reflected in his eyes.

"He never talks during *SpongeBob*," says Leroy.

I follow Leroy to the kitchen, where he boosts himself up on the counter. His legs hang way down. He waits for me to talk.

"Uh…Ben says you know how to write checks."

"Yeah?" Leroy crosses his arms. "So?"

"Can you show me how? I need to write some."

"You thinking about ripping off your folks?"

"Nah. Nothing like that. It's just that the bills are piling up. My dad's been away for a while."

"I know about that," he says. "Mine holds the record." He springs down from the counter. The checkbook he takes out of the drawer by the sink has a brown plastic cover. He flips it open and grabs the pen that's tucked in the fold. The checks say Julia Mae Gibbs on the top.

"First you gotta date the check." He clicks out the pen point and writes.

"Wait a second, that date's the end of next week."

"That's when Mom gets paid." He pulls an envelope from the utility company out of the same drawer and opens it. "Look for the 'pay to' line on your bill. Like here it says 'City of Tallahassee'." He writes that on the check. "Look for the total due, that's here."

I notice that the Gibbs owe a lot less than we do—maybe that's why they keep most of their lights out.

"You write that number here and here. On this line you spell it out. On this one you write it in numbers. Do the cents as a fraction, like this: 72/100. And then you sign it." He writes out *Julia Mae Gibbs* in cursive.

"You can do that? Fake her signature?"

"It's not her signature."

"What if they notice?"

Leroy has light blue eyes like you hardly ever see on black guys. His stare is icy. "You think bankers have time to sit around looking at signatures?"

"I don't know...it's their job, isn't it?"

He flips to the front of the checkbook. "Don't forget to write the amount in the ledger and subtract it from the balance. Just 'cause you have checks doesn't mean you have money to cover."

"What happens if I write a check and I don't have enough? I mean—"

He holds up his hand. "Man, don't even go there. You write a check and it bounces, they slam you with all kinds of fees." He takes a kettle off the stove and walks over to the sink.

"But how can they charge you if you don't have enough in there to begin with?"

He's filling the kettle, but gives me a look. "They got ways." He reaches over and pushes me. "Now, get out of here. My mom'll be home in a few. She doesn't want to see you crowding up her kitchen. All she wants is a cup of instant and to put her feet up."

"Thanks, Leroy." When I walk by Jahmal I say, "Give my regards to SpongeBob." The kid doesn't even blink.

O

"How about some popcorn, Mom?"

"Shhh..." She hangs on the commentator's every word: *And now the president is being greeted by his colleagues from the House and Senate.*

"Come on, Mom. I'm nervous, you're nervous; popcorn will help."

"Shush. He's about to speak."

"No he isn't. He's getting backslapped by bald guys in suits. Call me when he mentions Iraq."

I go in the kitchen and nuke a bag of Pop Secret. It takes a few minutes, but Mom doesn't call me. Steaming popcorn bag in hand, I roll over the back of the couch and land beside her. "Anything on Iraq yet?"

She shakes her head no. "He's talking about Afghanistan."

Afghanistan has nothing to do with us, or Duane, or anyone we know. I pull the bag open. Hot steam hits my face. "Maybe the news guys have been blowing the Iraq thing all out of proportion. Maybe the prez is cool on Iraq."

But Mom, who is teetering on the edge of the sofa, demands, "What about Iraq?" She grabs a piece of popcorn and flips it at the set, but it falls short.

"Yeah," I say, getting into it. "What about Iraq?" I launch a second popcorn missile. When it hits him on the eyebrow, Mom and I cheer. She helps herself to more popcorn, nibbling on a few kernels.

For each topic he brings up that isn't Iraq, the prez takes another hit. *Ping.* After Mom's first miss we go six for six. "Maybe we should quit," she says. "It's kind of disrespectful."

"Relax, Mom. The president isn't *really* inside that little box." She swats my arm.

I'm lining up my next shot when the prez says the magic word, Iraq.

I put the round of ammo in my mouth and chew slowly. Mom squeezes the edge of the sofa with buttery hands.

Once he's on the subject, the president names all our fears: Saddam has anthrax by the truckload; something called botulinum toxin too, enough to kill millions.

"I can see why you want to take this guy out," I tell the prez, "but do you have to send Duane to do it?" Mom looks really scared so I point out, "Duane's as far from the Persian Gulf as we are, Mom."

Just then the president leans into our living room. "Tonight I have a message for the men and women who will keep the peace, members of the American armed forces…"

I wonder if Duane and his buddies are watching, leaning toward the set.

"…the success of our cause will depend on you. Your training has prepared you. Your honor will guide you. You believe in America, and America believes in you."

Mom reaches over, grabs my hand and holds on. She doesn't let go until the president wraps things up.

"And may God continue to bless the United States of America." "But wait…" says Mom as the men in suits stand and clap. "Did he say that he's sending the troops in?"

"Umm…I don't think so."

We watch the post-speech rundown to see what the experts think. They don't know either. Half an hour later the phone rings. It's Mr. MasterCard. I answer his "Hi, Jus" with a flat "Hi, Dad" and pass the phone to Mom. I don't want to talk to him.

"What did you think?" she asks him. "Is he sending the troops to Iraq?" She hangs on every word, like Dad has some inside line to the White House. "I know, I know," she says, apologetically. "He's got a job to do—I'm proud of him too." She wipes her eyes with her wrist and whispers, "But I'm his mother. I want him to be safe."

They're still talking when I retreat to Duane's room. I sleep here pretty often these days. My own room is turning into a laundry dump. Before closing Duane's door, I pull my sweatshirt off over my head, ball it up, and launch it across the hall. The shirt unwinds as it flies. It hangs itself up on the floor. I look at my brother's chin-up bar but don't touch it. Instead, I close the door and sit down hard on his bed.

Nothing's right anymore. I mean, the room is better than any place else, but it's like the walls are getting thin.

Something furry butts me in the ribs. I pick up Duane's

scrawny old cat and lie back on the bed. Giz settles in the middle of my chest. In the light from the bedside lamp I see the iridescent blue of the cataracts on his eyes. In a second his eyes squeeze shut. He curls his front paws under him and begins to purr. Feeling the deep rumble in my chest, I reach for the recorder.

Hey, Jus—

I got your letter about the breathing problem. This is a very big tip: Do not—repeat—do not let a girl know she is giving you a breathing problem—tell her you have asthma.

A related tip: Do not sweat, stutter, or change color around a girl. And never ever tell a girl you like her. Let her say it first.

Not much going on here—just the usual. I scared myself bad on the rifle range today. The targets were popping up. First shot—my M16 malfunctioned. I squeezed the trigger and heard a click. It happens. You break it down, you troubleshoot it. No biggie. Only this time my hands start shaking. I'm thinking this could happen in a live-fire situation in Iraq. While I mess with my rifle, they're shooting at me.

Don't get too worried. All the guys are jumpy—I'll be fine. I'm just mouthing off.

Remember to keep breathing. I will too.

Duane

We walk home as a group. Jemmie and I follow Ben and Cass—who have definitely gotten over their big fight. Leroy circles us, popping wheelies. Back at the school, he offered Jemmie a lift. "Come on, girl, stand on the pegs." But she turned him down.

Still trying to impress her, he does lame tricks all the way to the girls' houses. It's kind of sad the way he never gives up.

He plants both feet and leans on the handlebars as Jemmie marches up her walk. "What's wrong with her? PMS?" But the slamming door has nothing to do with him. It's for Cass, who doesn't even notice.

When she's with Ben, Cass's world shrinks. The only thing in it is Ben.

The happy couple drifts up the walk to the Bodines' house—a parent-approved arrangement because there's an "adult" in the house. Whoever decided that Cass's older sister Lou Ann qualified as an adult doesn't know Lou Ann very well.

Leroy stands on the pedals. "Later, Lard." The bike rocks side to side between his thighs as he rides away. His little brother gets off school twenty minutes before we do. Until his mom comes home from her job at the Waffle House, Leroy's the adult at his place.

I go on alone. A couple of houses down, I pass the end of a driveway with half a dozen newspapers in it, all turning yellow from the sun. Sometimes the man who lives there, Mr. Barnett, disappears into his house for days at a time. Duane says that, as a POW in Vietnam, Mr. Barnett was tortured; that's why he acts strange.

I'm just past his yard when I hear a hoarse voice say, "Hey, Justin. Got a minute?" Mr. Barnett has just stepped out on the house's narrow concrete porch.

"Want me to bring your papers?" I ask.

"Don't bother." He lowers himself into a folding chair. "I already got more news than I can handle."

I trot across his patchy lawn. "You okay, Mr. Barnett?" He looks pale and damp, like something that's soaked in water too long.

"Just dandy," he says. "Have a seat." He uses the cigarette in his hand to point out a chair. "Killer! Lillian!" he snaps at the Chihuahuas who are barking and bulging the screen with their faces. "Shut the heck up!"

He swings one toothpick leg over the other. The black corduroy slipper on his dangling foot twitches up and down. I wait for him to start talking. Duane knows him real well; he used to cut his lawn. Afterwards, they'd sit down and talk, sometimes for hours. But I don't really know him.

"Wanted to ask you about Duane," he finally rasps. His red eyes dart to my right shoulder, the front of my shirt, my left shoe, the road, and finally to a speck on the knee of his pants that isn't even there. He picks it off anyway. "Is Duane gonna get thrown into this mess of a war we got coming?"

"It kind of looks like it."

"Sheee-it." He uncrosses his legs and hunches forward. He rests his forearms on his thighs. For a minute he just slumps, as if someone's kicked out his plug.

"It still might not happen," I offer.

His head jerks up. He stares into my eyes. "Don't kid yourself, son. We got too many men and too much ordnance over there already. It's gonna happen."

"It'll be quick though, right? We have better weapons than they do. I mean, we're the superpower. Who are they?"

"Who are *they*?" His voice cracks. "*Who are they?* I'll tell you who *they* are. They're the guys who hide behind trees and take our boys out one by one by one—that's who they are."

"But there aren't any trees in Iraq except for, like, a couple of palms. It's a desert."

"Then they shoot from the windows of a school, or they come up with their hands in the air and dynamite strapped to their bodies under those bathrobes they wear. Maybe that's how they kill us this time." His breath smells like cigarettes. "Does it matter? Dead is dead."

"But...but...we'll be in and out of there..." My voice trails off.

He prods my chest with a finger. "Let me tell you, son, nothing's easier to get into than a war. And nothing's harder to get out of." His words swarm out like fire ants when you poke their mound with a stick. "Give Duane a message from me. Tell him, don't play hero. You got that? Tell him to stay alive. And one more thing. Tell him, don't expect no parades when he comes home." Suddenly, he stands and jerks the door open so fast the dogs spring back. "America gets tired of its wars real fast these days. Tired of its soldiers too." He slams the door behind him.

When I stand, my pack feels heavier, my legs tired and slow. I can hardly drag myself home.

○

As soon as I get to the house I make a beeline for the half gallon of Rocky Road Mom hid behind a box of spinach. I rinse a spoon, then park my butt on the couch. I dig into the ice cream like it's a wall and Duane's on the other side.

The Giz climbs up next to me and licks the flopped-open lid. "Very sanitary, Giz." But I don't stop him. Before I put the box away behind the spinach, I make sure that the ice cream is eaten down far enough so the lid doesn't touch.

I fall back on the sofa with a groan. I should never have eaten so much. But why did Mr. Barnett have to tell me all that crap? I close my eyes and try to concentrate on the whoosh of the air coming out of the heat register over my head. I pretend like it's the wind blowing and I'm someplace a billion miles from here.

I'm halfway into the Big Nothing when the Giz steps up on my chest and begins to knead the front of my shirt with his paws. "Ow, ow, ow!" His claws are like little hypodermic needles. I jump up and rescue my spoon from the sink and stand with my head in the freezer, wolfing Rocky Road.

I hate what I'm doing—I can practically feel myself blimp—but a spoon and a carton of Rocky Road are pretty much all I have. Hey, you work with what you've got.

Then I remember the bills on the coffee table, waiting to be paid. That's something I can do.

I dig through a couple of drawers in Dad's desk afraid he took the checkbook with him. I'm about to give up when I find it in the bottom drawer.

I pay the utility bill first, doing it the way Leroy showed me. I take a deep breath and launch into Dad's signature. I make the J pointy. So far so good. It looks very Dad. I let the last g and the s in Riggs flatline the way he does, but it doesn't look right.

"Pretty unconvincing," I mutter. "I hope you're right about the bank guys, Leroy."

The bill has two halves. One says "return with payment." I stuff it in the envelope along with the check. The other says "retain for your records." I don't know where Dad keeps our records. I start a pile of my own.

I lick the flap and mash it down, then realize there's no address in the little window. I must've put the bill in backwards. I peel the flap back up and turn the bill around, but now the flap doesn't want to stick. I have to tape it.

Then I remember about the ledger at the front of the checkbook. I flip to it, ready to add my check to Dad's list and subtract it from the balance. Instead I stare. The ledger is blank. Dad hasn't kept track of a single check—which means there's no way to tell how much money's in the account. "Slick move, Dad. If this check bounces, it's your butt, not mine."

But whose butt is it if he never comes back? Mom doesn't make enough by herself to cover the bills. Mom's job is OPS. I don't know what it stands for, only that it means she's not permanent, doesn't have benefits, and doesn't make much.

I slide out the MasterCard bill and look at the total. How do I know Dad has eight hundred and thirty-two dollars in the account? If I pay it then maybe all the checks will bounce. Mom and I need the lights to stay on.

Then I notice there's a box that says minimum payment due: forty-three dollars. I call Leroy.

"Yeah," he says. "That's what you're supposed to pay. The minimum." I tear up the first check and fill out another one for the minimum.

I write six checks and record every one of them in the ledger. Then I sit back, exhausted. On one side of the desk I have the sealed envelopes, on the other, the halves of each bill for my records. I put five of those in a drawer, but there's one I don't want for my records—the one that got me into the bill-paying business in the first place.

I take the MasterCard bill over to the stove and turn on the flame. All Dad's charges begin to curl up black and flake into the burner.

Wah wah wah, a piercing sound fills the room. I drop the flaming paper. "What the…?" A smoke detector I've never seen before is squealing its brains out over the kitchen door.

I'm standing on a chair trying to weasel the batteries out of it when Mom walks in. She covers her heart with her hand. "Justin, not again!"

I manage to pop the batteries out and the kitchen goes silent. "Mom, it's not what you think!" When I was a little kid I was sort of a pyro. I incinerated a bunch of stuff in our driveway—I kept stealing Dad's lighter.

She walks over to the stove and stares at the ashes. "If this is a report card you're in big trouble."

"It's not a report card. And since when did we get a smoke detector?"

"I put it up a couple of days ago. Is this a note from a girl?"

I can tell she likes the idea so I say, "Could be. Now, why did you put up a smoke detector?"

"I'm a mom. It's my responsibility to keep you safe—is she nice?"

"Is who nice?"

"The girl who wrote you the note." She drifts to the fridge and opens the freezer door. I don't realize what she's doing until she moves the spinach aside. She's picked a bad time to start craving ice cream.

"Justin?" All thoughts about the mystery girl who supposedly sent me a note have left her brain. She stares into the Rocky Road carton. It holds barely enough for one good bowl. "Tell me you didn't eat this all by yourself."

"Would it make a difference if I told you the Giz helped?"

"You really *are* in trouble now." She picks up a spoon and

digs in. "The girl who sent the note isn't going to like it either. Take it from someone who knows: nobody likes fat." She lectures me while she polishes off the rest of the half gallon. After scraping the sides with the spoon she lets Giz lick the carton. We don't have any willpower in this house. None.

To make up for it we eat lettuce and tomato salads for dinner, with a little tuna crumbled on top, like good calories are the antidote to bad ones.

"How was your day?" Mom asks out of the blue.

I've been thinking about Mr. Barnett's rant about guys shooting at Duane, so the "how was your day?" takes me by surprise. I give her the shrug-off.

She imitates my shrug. "Seriously, tell me one thing that happened to you today."

"Mo-om…" We used to take turns at the dinner table. Each of us had to say one thing that had happened to us during the day. "C'mon, Mom. It's just the two of us."

She pushes a lettuce leaf around with her fork. "Two is still a family, Justin."

"O-kay… So, I guess the thing that happened to me was the note."

"You going to tell me who she is?" Her cheeks look kind of pink. This is weird; Mom is blushing.

I make up all this crap about how this mystery girl in my English class really likes me. To me it sounds far-fetched, but Mom enjoys the heck out of it. I let her pester me a while, but I never crack, never name names. Finally I hold up my hands. "Enough about the note! It's your turn. Tell me one thing that happened to you today."

"Nothing *happen*-happened. But I took a look at online job listings. What do you think, Jus? Should I try for something better?" She seems hopeful for about a second, and then she wilts as if she's already tried and been turned down. "Too bad all I have is a GED…"

"And experience, Mom. You have experience. Plus you're good. You should try."

"Maybe sometime," she says and she takes a sip of cold coffee left over from breakfast.

"You could do it, Mom, really." Mom is more afraid of trying than she is of having a bad job for the rest of her life. It's like me and Jemmie Lewis. I'll definitely ask Jemmie out—sometime.

"Are you up for a video?" I ask.

"My pick?"

I was hoping we might actually go out and rent a movie made in my lifetime, but Mom is headed for the couch. "It's my turn," I insist, trailing her. "You picked last time."

"I'm the grown-up!"

"So…be nice to the kid!"

We do rock, paper, scissors. In the final round Mom's paper covers my rock, so we watch *The African Queen*, which I've only seen, like, a dozen times.

Humphrey Bogart again. In this one he plays a sloppy loser, an old geezer who needs a shave as bad as Mr. Barnett. But the woman he's transporting in his junker boat, the *African Queen*, falls for him—probably because he's the only guy within a hundred million miles who isn't a Nazi. At the end they sink a German ship, but most of the time it's just the two of them on the boat, drifting around. They don't even like each other at first, but by the end they're practically making out.

I sit there half watching, half not. I wonder what a note from Jemmie would say, if she wrote me one? Probably something like: *What's the algebra homework, Big?*

What I need is the same opportunity as Bogart in *The*

African Queen. If it were just the two of us, Jemmie might find something about me that she liked, something she never noticed when there were so many distractions—like other guys—around.

I'm still trying to decide what that "something" might be when the movie ends. Before Mom can switch to CNN I take the zanger out of her hand and turn off the TV. "Come on, Mom. Time for bed." I herd her toward the stairs. "By the way, I paid the bills."

She stalls on the staircase and turns toward me. "You know how to pay bills?"

"Sure. They go over it in school." I don't want to mention my lesson in the Gibbs's kitchen.

"I'm so sorry, Justin. I should be worrying about the bills—not you. I'm the mother."

"It's no big deal." I take her by the shoulders and start her marching again. "It's good practice for later."

When we reach the hall she turns on the light and looks at me hard. "You're a good kid, Jus."

"You're right, I am. And you're a good mom."

She grabs my arm and kisses me on the ear—a direct hit. "Go easy on the eardrum, Mom!" I give her a quick hug, then dive into Duane's room and close the door, my ear still ringing.

Dear Duane,

   Undisputable truth: You can't eat 92% of a carton of Rocky Road without activating the zit machine. I tried it Thursday night. When I woke up the next morning I looked like I'd run into a swarm of bees. I did the whole scrub and medicate thing. It only got the zits angry.
   I hid out all weekend. Saturday night Mom and I staged a raid on Taco Bell, but that was about it. I played the keyboard and a mess of video games—got plenty of finger exercise. Now it's Monday. The face is still bad so I'm about to fake a stomachache. I can't make that throw-up sound as good as you but I'll try. Wish me luck.

                    Your sick brother,
                    Justin

Uhhh… My stomach still feels queasy." I try to sound pitiful.

"Your stomach is fine." Mom's look says, *I know you weren't sick yesterday when I let you stay home, so don't push it.* "Your face is fine too. You're just self conscious."

"What about this zit? It's so big it needs its own zip code."

"That little thing? No one will even notice it." She offers me some gloppy cover-up cream, but I won't touch it. I have *some* pride.

On my way to school I find a quarter and a number two pencil. I'm so busy watching the ground, I don't notice Jemmie and Leroy walking a little way ahead of me until they start talking.

"How come you don't like me?" Leroy asks.

"Quit bugging me. I like you fine."

"You do?" He drifts a little closer to her.

Sad to say, but they look good together. He's taller than her, not just a little, but inches. From the back their braids almost match. He lets his arm swing out so his knuckles brush the back of her hand.

She pulls away, but not as quick as I thought she would. He must feel the difference too. He turns and steps in front of her. He walks slower and slower, the distance between them shrinking until it feels like something's going to happen. I yell, "Hey, Leroy."

His strange blue eyes stare over her head. "Can't you see I'm busy, Lard?"

"Morning, Big Rig!" Jemmie knows it's me without even looking. She turns on Leroy. "Leroy, you're such a jerk."

"A jerk?" Leroy looks confused.

"Only a jerk calls a friend Lard." She cuts around him and takes off.

Then it's just Leroy and me, facing each other in the road. His skinny shoulders lift, then drop. "Girls."

"Yeah, girls," I agree. "Go figure." We walk the rest of the way in silence.

○

I spend the day studying the top of my desk. Ditto the floor when I'm changing classes—I'm getting to know the stains on the linoleum better than the janitors. I don't talk to Jemmie. I don't want her to look at my face and lose her lunch.

Leaving school, I'm counting dried-up globs of who-knows-what on the pavement when I hear Jemmie say, "Fine with me, Cass. Wait for Ben. I'm going home with Cherise anyway." I glance up and take a quick snapshot of the scene and look down again.

Cherise, who's about as tall as Cass and Jemmie, but heavier, has an arm around Jemmie's shoulders. Cherise's straightened hair is bleached orange. She dates a football player from Rickards High named Antoine Greer. Guys at Monroe Middle think she's scary.

"Jemmie?" Cass says quietly. "Can I talk to you a minute? Alone."

Another quick look shows Jemmie unwinding Cherise's arm from around her neck. "Be right back, Cher." As Jemmie and Cass walk toward me, I drop my pack on the ground and open it like I'm checking something. When they stop they're almost on top of me. My eyes are even with Jemmie's knees and the lower edge of Cass's skirt—Cass has undergone a weird, skirt-wearing conversion since she and Ben started going together. Even though it's cold, Jemmie sticks stubbornly to their old uniform, shorts and a T-shirt. Looks like Jemmie's been scratching her knees again.

"I'm not stopping you." Cass twines one bare white leg around the other. "I mean, it's okay if you hang out with Cherise sometimes, but we're still best friends, aren't we?"

Jemmie's sneakers are wide apart. The left one ticks from the sole to the side of the shoe, over and over.

"Jemmie," Cherise calls. "You coming, girl?"

The left shoe rocks onto its side one last time, then Jemmie plants it and pivots. "See ya later, Cass." She trots over to Cherise and they take off.

The next thing I hear is Cass crying. Three girls rush over to comfort her. The backs of their white knees flex and sway as they talk softly to her. I crawl a couple of feet, dragging my pack. As soon as I clear the leg forest I scramble to my feet. I'm jamming an arm under a pack strap when a voice says, "Hey, Jus." Ben stands off to one side of the girl pileup. He must have just walked out of the school; bet he wishes he hadn't.

I hold out a hand for him to slap. "Let's go, man. She'll catch up."

He doesn't even see the hand. "That's okay. Think I'll wait."

O

Nana Grace squints at me through the glare on the storm door. "Hello, Justin Riggs." I drum my fingers on the spot where Artie's face is smooshed against the glass. He giggles. Nana pushes the door open. "It ain't Wednesday yet, is it?"

"No, ma'am, but Jemmie's at Cherise Williams's house."

"First I heard about it." Nana swings Artie up on her hip. "That girl better check in."

"Um, would it be all right if I play the piano for a few minutes?"

"Sure. Be my guest."

When I open the lid a soft *boom* travels along the piano strings. I have the feeling that Mr. Sohmer has been waiting for me.

I let my right hand wander, finding a melody about a kid who watched the ground all day. Definitely minor.

The phone rings. Probably Jemmie checking in. My left hand tries a chord. I depress the pedal and feel it throb. My throat gets thick. Great. I'm only a couple of chords away from tears. I kick the tune into a major key. Maybe Mr. Sohmer can talk me out of feeling lousy.

Nana sets a glass of milk and a plate of cookies on the piano. Her hand rests on my shoulder. "How'd you get so much sad in you?" she asks. She squeezes my shoulder to let me know she doesn't really expect an answer. "Go on. Play."

And so I play, following a tune in my head. As I lean into the piano, I feel like I'm dipping the music out like water.

I haven't been playing long when the front door opens with a bang, then slams shut, and Jemmie stomps up the stairs.

Nana Grace comes out of the kitchen, towel over her shoulder. "Jemmeal?" She stares up the steps after her granddaughter. "What's the matter, child?" Upstairs, a second door slams.

"She's sad," I say, not looking up from the piano.

"Well, you got that right," Nana Grace agrees. "Not a thing we can do about it, though. Those two girls gotta work it out themselves." She goes back in the kitchen, shaking her head.

· After that I play for Jemmie. It's a safe thing to do since she probably doesn't hear me.

I find a string of notes that sounds like the sun breaking through clouds. I play it again, and again. I get so caught up I don't hear the knock on the door. All I hear is Nana crossing the room behind me, the soles of her sneakers keeping time with my playing.

"Well, look who's here. Cass Bodine. Come on in, stranger."

My fingers instantly turn stupid. But Cass doesn't notice me. She throws herself at Nana Grace. Artie throws himself at the backs of Cass's legs and hangs on.

"Oh, Nana, what am I going to do?" Cass is crying again—assuming she ever stopped. I stare at the keys. Prickles stab the back of my neck. Boy, am I ever in the wrong place.

"She doesn't like me anymore," Cass moans.

"Oh, yes she does. She surely does. But it's not me you need to talk to. The one you need to talk to is up them stairs."

"She's home?" I hear Cass snuff like she's trying to get snot to go the other way. "I thought she went to Cherise's."

"She went, and now she's back. Here, have a hankie."

Cass blows loudly. "Can you come with me, please?"

"Me," says Artie. "I'll come."

"Oh, no you won't either," says Nana. "Let's go read a book. Cass has got to go up them stairs by herself."

I catch them out of the corner of my eye when they walk to the stairs. A tear drips off Cass's chin. "Go on, now," says Nana Grace. "She's been waitin' for you."

Cass tiptoes up the steps. I hear a timid knock. "Jemmie?"

I close the piano lid, but the melody I was playing keeps making itself up inside my head. I wish I could sit back down and play it just one more time, but with the house full of traumatized girls, it's time to go.

The music trails me home. It's like the soundtrack of my life, the movie. As I walk it shifts minor again. I might be the star of this movie, but it's a sad one.

I open the door thinking french fries. I remember what Mom said about no one liking fat. But fat or thin, it's not like anyone notices me anyway.

I turn on the stove, dump a bag of frozen fries onto a cookie sheet, and slide the sheet into the oven.

My theme music is beginning to fade. "Listen to this," I tell the Giz. Desperate to hang on to it, I play it on the edge of the table, humming along, and it kind of comes back. "It's in the fingers, Giz. I'm the guy with music in his fingers." The Giz yawns so big his tongue curls.

By the time the smell of fries begins to fill the kitchen, the melody is gone. I feel real empty, so I make up something stupid to fill the hole.

"*Fry* heaven, *fry* heaven," I sing to the cat. "The kitchen smells like *fry* heaven. Grease and salt and potato slabs..." But the only thing that rhymes is flabby abs.

I put on an oven mitt. I'm pulling the fries out when I hear the knock. Three quick, two slow. I open the front door with the cookie sheet in my hand. Ben lifts his head and sniffs. A smile breaks over his face. "Fries. All right!"

While we stuff our faces he tells me about Cass going over to Jemmie's to talk to Nana Grace.

"Jemmie's there too—I mean I think she is. I saw her walk by."

"I hope she goes easy on Cass. You know how Jemmie is." Ben ducks under the table, suddenly all interested in tying a shoelace. "Cass says Jemmie kind of liked me, you know, before the two of us got together."

"Liked you? Wait—are you saying Jemmie's mad at Cass because she's jealous?"

Ben comes back up slowly. "Uh...maybe at first. She doesn't like me anymore. I think she's getting into Leroy now."

"You've got to be kidding." I feel as if I'm imploding, but I act like it's a big joke. "Why would she go from dumb to desperate?"

Ben picks up another fry. "Wonder how it's going over there? I bet they've made up and everything's okay."

"Or else Jemmie's chucking all the goofy little things Cass ever gave her over to Cass's side of the fence: end of friendship."

Ben groans. "If Jemmie dumps Cass she'll be all over me crying again."

"I bleed for you, man. It must be hard having a girl all over you."

"Oh yeah, it is." His grin says he's lying. But the smile fades. "She's afraid she'll lose Jemmie as a best friend. Listen," he mumbles, "I don't want to lose you as a best friend either."

This is my chance to say how I feel. This is my chance to talk.

"You think these need more ketchup?" I ask.

He passes me the bottle. "Sure. You do the honors."

I squeeze the bottle from an overhead position, making squiggly loops on what's left of the pile.

For a moment a little of my movie music comes back. Accompanied by the burp of squirting ketchup, it sounds funny and sad, sort of like circus music.

Yo, Jus—

You threw me a curve about Jemmie. (I know I turn everything into baseball—but one day you'll figure out that everything is baseball.) I didn't think you liked girls that way. I guess you're growing up. (Next time I'm home you can punch me for saying that.)

At your age I was in love with Melissa Betts. Remember her from that day we ran into her at Wakulla Springs and you said there should be a law about who could buy a bikini? You have to take my word for it—she was cute in 8th.

What I'm saying is don't worry if things don't work out with Jemmie. Think of her as practice. Even if she breaks your heart, you might be glad later (think about Melissa Betts in her bikini).

One more girl-getting tip: Girls change their minds a lot. They don't always say what they mean or mean what they say. They get confused. It doesn't hurt to help them make up their minds.

Happy hunting! (See—I didn't even mention baseball.)

Duane

We sit side by side on my porch steps and stare into the yard. "Come on, Big." Jemmie bumps my knee with hers. "This is simple. All I asked was, what do you think of him? Objective opinion."

"Objective, subjective…I didn't listen real well the day Butler gave that lecture. Objective is the one that comes from your head, not your gut, right?"

"Uh-huh."

"An objective opinion about Leroy Gibbs…hmmm." I try to keep my voice smooth, but when it comes to Leroy—Leroy and her—I can't be objective. Being objective is for things that don't matter. "Well, I guess it depends."

Suddenly, her skinny arm is around my neck. "What's it depend on?" The arm squeezes.

"Hey! You're strangling me!" I squeak. Maybe she'll laugh and forget the question. The choke hold tightens. "Okay, okay; I'll talk." I rub my windpipe.

"All right," I say. "Leroy Gibbs. Objective opinion. I guess it depends on what you're looking for. If we're talking basketball I'd say, yeah, I'd want him on my side. A bike race, I'd pick Ben or Clay over him. Now, if you're scoring him on clothes? On a scale of one to ten, Leroy's are a negative four."

She leans forward and stares at my sneakers. "Where's that put these kicks, Big?"

My socks are welling out the sides of my shoes. The sneakers are so dirty it's hard to guess the original color. "A negative twenty-seven?" I joke. "Time to get out the old duct tape." I pull my feet in toward the step.

"You still haven't told me what you think of him."

"What have I just been doing? Aren't you listening?"

"As a *boyfriend*, Big. What do you think of him as a boyfriend?"

"Not my type," I mutter.

She pinches my arm hard. "For me, Big, a boyfriend for me!"

I almost say, *Excuse me, I have to go jump off the roof now.* "I don't know," I mumble. "I guess he's okay." Much as I hate to admit it, Leroy *is* okay.

She blows out hard and flops back, locking her hands behind her head. I flop back too.

We watch a wasp bump along the porch ceiling, dazed by the cold. "I don't like him that much," she says, staring up. "Sure, he's cute. Really, really, really cute."

"You're making me gag."

"Sorry, I'm making myself gag too."

"What do you think of Ben? Is he really, really, really, really cute?"

"Ben? I don't like *him!* He's going with my best friend!" The wasp finally bumbles his way out from under the edge of the roof and flies off. "Why do I have to date anyway?" she complains. "Guys are so gross!"

"Hey, you don't need to tell me about it! I know. I am one."

Her head turns. "You're not gross, you're nice."

She's looking into my eyes and telling me I'm nice. "I am *not* nice! Get to know me better, I'm really not." Nice is the exact opposite of boyfriend. To her I'm a girl. I'm doomed.

She sits up fast and jerks the string on her sweatshirt hood back and forth until the hood is all bunched up. "What am I going to do, Big? Ben and Cass want me to go places with them all the time. I hate tagging along. They asked me to go to the movies with them tomorrow night."

"So, eat some popcorn, enjoy the show…"

"It's a *date*, Big. I'm not going on a date with them—especially not on Valentine's."

All of a sudden, a voice inside my head that sounds a lot like Duane's says, *This is it, kid. Help her make up her mind. Don't blow it.*

I sit back up and spread my arms. "Ideal solution. Me. The *un*date. I go places with you, but I don't slob all over you like Leroy. This would be strictly professional."

"Professional, like I'd have to pay you? Forget that."

"No, no. I mean—I assume we'd be going cool places, right?"

"Tomorrow night we're going to the dollar movie." She gives me a level look. "Pretty cool, huh?"

"You're in luck. I like movies." I lean back on my arms. "And I think I'm available tomorrow night. So, what do you say? Is it an undate?" If she had X-ray vision she'd see my heart is giving itself whiplash. "Either way is fine with me."

"I don't know, Big." She crosses her legs, swings her foot a couple of times, then tucks it behind her calf, twisting one leg around the other. Next she hugs herself so tight her fingers almost touch in back. Thinking about not dating me is turning her into a pretzel. "Why did Cass have to go and change?" she says. "She's such a wimp since she started going with Ben."

"Ben too. He's wimped out big time."

She turns and looks at me, one of those deep looks that might mean something. If I could make my mouth work now would be the time to mention her pretty eyes.

Good thing I don't, because when she opens her mouth

again I realize the deep look meant something else. "I couldn't stand it if you got weird on me too, Big," she says.

"Weird how?"

"Oh, you know…" She looks away again.

"Wait. You don't think I'd start *liking* you?" I make it sound as if I'd rather have monkeys fly out my butt. Meanwhile my heart is rattling its cage, screaming, *Tell her, tell her.*

Luckily the head is in charge. "So," I say, beaming indifference, "what are we going to see?"

"Something old and bad. You really want to do this?"

"Sure. I owe you."

"Owe me for what?"

"Uh…you let me play your piano?"

"Shoot, Big, I'll *give* you the piano. I'll help you push it over to your house." Then, *sproing,* her legs are in the locked and upright position. She dashes down the steps but stops at the end of the path and points a finger. "Okay," she yells back. "But this is *not* a date; we each pay our own share. That way we won't wreck things."

"Right!" I yell after her. "Why take a chance?"

The voice in my head says, *Way to go, little bro. Got yourself a date and it won't cost a nickel.*

Dear Duane,

News Flash! Jemmie and I are going on an undate. Never heard of an undate? It's like a date from the land of opposites.

What do you wear on an undate? I don't know. I don't know what you wear on a date either. I'm kind of new at this. I wish you were here for advice.

Jus

It isn't like Mom to get up spontaneously—especially since Dad left—but the one day I want her to stay in bed, she gets herself up and wanders into my room. The light-blocking mask she wears to help her sleep is pushed up on her forehead. Her hair pooches out above it like a lightbulb.

"Justin, what are you doing?" She doesn't seem to recognize the ironing board.

"Ow! Thanks, Mom. You made me burn my thumb. I'm ironing a T-shirt."

"Is it picture day?" She looks anxious. "If it's picture day you need a dress shirt with a button-down collar. Want me to iron one for you?"

"It's not picture day, Mom. The shirt's for later." The last thing I need is to show up for my undate in a button-down collar.

Mom smooths the wrinkle I just pressed into a sleeve. "What's happening later?"

"I have an undate with Jemmie Lewis. We're going to the movies with Ben and Cass."

"Is she the one who wrote you the note?"

"Jemmie? No way. That was someone else."

"I don't know about this, Justin. You're a little young to date…"

"It's an *un*date, Mom." I press another wrinkle into the sleeve.

"Will there be a chaperone?"

"Mo-om... Undates are like G movies. Nothing happens."

She stands up a little straighter in her old robe. "Will there be a chaperone?"

"You're taking your mother-job too seriously." I hold up my free hand. "Okay, okay. I'll bring Giz if you want. He's ninety-eight in human years."

Mom has a hard time processing information first thing in the morning. "Jemmie Lewis?" she says, rewinding in her head. "Isn't she kind of popular? Plus she's black, not that it matters to me. But other people...sometimes...well..." Her voice fades.

"Earth to Mom: it is *not* a date." I mush the label flat with the point of the iron, but it springs right back up.

"Here, let me." Suddenly all efficient, she takes charge of the iron. She opens the shirt, hangs it over the board, and irons it one layer at a time.

"Just go after the major wrinkles, Mom." But when she finishes and puts it on a hanger, it looks like T-shirt of the Gods. Rays of light practically shoot off it.

"Are you wearing your black pants with that?" She's still holding the iron.

"Jeans."

"Want me to press them?"

"No, Mom. Nobody irons jeans."

"Nobody irons T-shirts either."

"Yeah...well, thanks for doing the shirt. It looks great."

I go downstairs to fix breakfast and find a valentine on the table with my name on it. I open the envelope. Someone at Hallmark wrote: *For a sweetheart of a son, from Mom.* Mom personalized it by adding "the female Parental Unit." I feel bad that I didn't get her a valentine. She's obviously not going to get one from Dad. It's too late for breakfast in bed, which is what Duane and I used to do for her on special occasions, but at least I can fix her eggs instead of setting out the usual milk and dry cereal.

Mom comes to the table. While she was on a roll with the iron she must have pressed her skirt and blouse. She looks better than she has since Dad left. "Looking good, Mom."

"Thank you, Jus." She stares at the pile of greasy black eggs I slide onto her plate.

"Sorry. The margarine kind of burned."

She picks up her fork. "I'm sure they'll be delicious."

I give her a quick, one-arm hug. "Happy Valentine's, Mom."

O

Ben clutches his date's hand. As they gaze up at the marquee I notice that Ben's wearing a shirt with a button-down collar—looks like his mother got involved. I see why he can only afford the dollar movie—a bracelet with a heart-shaped charm on it circles Cass's wrist. It makes the string friendship bracelet from Jemmie that's under it look kind of ratty.

"What do you guys want to see?" Ben asks, but no one answers.

My undate is four feet away from me, wearing the same hoodie she had on yesterday. I should never have ironed the T-shirt.

Since nobody seems to want to make a choice I play emcee. "Today, ladies and gentlemen, our viewing choices include a war movie, a sci-fi flick—yeah, this is a good one. It features the extermination of all biological life on planet Earth!"

Cass pats her big hair with her free hand. Her sister, who has beauty school ambitions, must have fixed it for her. She seems self-conscious about it, asking Jemmie every ten minutes if it looks okay. "I don't want to see anything with blood," she says. "Sorry." Her hand goes to her hair again, trying to pat it down.

Ben gives me a suffering, apologetic look.

"O-kay. Survey says: blood is out. No war, no total annihilation." I scan our dwindling options. "Let's see. We have two choices in the romance department."

"Romance?" As Jemmie crosses her arms, the too-short sleeves of her sweatshirt ride up, showing off the friendship bracelet that matches Cass's. "Romances make me want to puke," she announces.

"All righty, then. That leaves…Jackie Chan."

Ben takes out his wallet and pays for Cass. Jemmie and I whip out our matching dollars.

Holding our tickets, we walk into a lobby painted a glossy blood red, like a Chinese restaurant. Our sneakers make little sticking sounds as we cross the lobby.

Black-and-white paintings of old movie stars watch us from the walls. They're so bad that even I, who have been well trained by Mom, have a hard time identifying them.

"Buy you popcorn?" I ask Jemmie. "Or is that off-limits on an undate?"

She shrugs. "Whatever."

I take that as a "yes" and buy the jumbo size.

"I'll get it next time," she says, meaning this isn't a date—but also implying there *will* be a next time. Yes!

"F and C?" I ask Ben.

"For kung fu? Definitely." We naturally head for the first row, center seats—the only place to be if you want to check out the tread on the sole of Jackie's shoe when he kicks.

I can tell that Jemmie agrees with Ben and me but Cass

prefers to sit further back. Jemmie goes along with her. Ben told me that the girls have worked things out. Even though it's hard, Jemmie is obviously trying to keep the worked-out feeling going. "You sure it looks okay?" Cass asks as we slide into a middle row. Jemmie reassures her for, like, the twenty-first time that her hair is fine.

We flop into seats: Ben, Cass, Jemmie, then me. The previews roll. They're for old-new movies, but the sound is loud and the picture is big. It almost makes up for the pukey smell coming from my seat. Actually, I don't mind it that much, but I complain to Jemmie about it so she doesn't think it's me.

Then it's Jackie time.

Unfortunately the film has a scratch that skips across the screen like a bolt of lightning.

"This is so lame," says Cass.

"It's probably just at the beginning," whispers Ben, the guy who couldn't afford two tickets to a real movie.

"Cass is right," says Jemmie. "Let's demand our money back."

"Here girls, have some popcorn." I plunk the tub in Jemmie's lap and watch the scratch, feeling the rhythm of its dits and dashes. *Da-dah, da-dah, da.*

Jemmie pinches my arm.

"Hey, is touching allowed on an undate?" I ask. But the pinch is to make me stop doing what I'm doing, which is drumming along with the scratch on the film. I jam my hands between the seat and my thighs and think of Butler with his pencils, drumming on his chair. I don't want to look like him.

I try to concentrate on Jackie, but the rhythm won't stop *da-dah*ing in my head. I play it with my fingers, pushing it into the seat cushion, then glance at Jemmie to see if I'm getting away with it.

I am—she doesn't notice me at all. She's watching Cass, who is watching Ben. Ben is focused on Jackie, one hundred percent. They form a chain of not-noticing.

There has to be some way to get Jemmie's attention.

Before my brain can get in the way I tug a hand out from under my thigh and do something Duane and I used to do.

I make an elephant.

My middle finger is the trunk; the other three fingers and thumb are legs.

When my brother and I did it, we were Ellie and Phantor, the battling pachyderms. We'd trunk-fight on the kitchen table until one of us knocked over a glass. Now I walk my lone elephant down my thigh. My elephant waves its trunk at Jemmie just as she turns away from Cass.

My brain is horrified. Making a finger elephant is bad enough, but what if she thinks my middle finger is supposed to be something other than a trunk?

Busted! She sees the elephant. She's staring. I can't read her face in the flickering light—but she's got to be thinking, this is my last undate with this fool.

Then suddenly there is a second elephant standing on *her* thigh, waving a trunk back at *me*. With Duane, my elephant was smaller than his; I was always Ellie. But Jemmie has girl hands, thin with long fingers. She is Ellie, definitely. And I am the undisputed heavyweight trunk-wrestling champ of the world—the mighty Phantor.

I don't have to explain to her about trunk-wrestling. Jemmie is so competitive that if Duane and I hadn't invented it, she would have. Now, a good trunk fight needs to be staged on solid ground. That's how we end up with our thighs mashed together, middle fingers locked in combat—and technically holding hands.

As we battle, I make an interesting discovery. When it comes to regular sports, I might be a wimp compared to Jemmie, but I have stronger, bigger hands. Phantor is whipping Ellie's butt when the woman in front of us swivels her fat neck and whispers loudly, "Do you two mind?"

"It's the elephants," I whisper back. "They're out of control." And I pull Jemmie to her feet by her trunk finger. "Come on. Let's get some drinks."

We laugh as we stumble down the aisle and through the doors to the lobby. The whole time our fingers stay locked. Before she can say something about finger-holding being a major violation of the rules of undating, I let go and join the line at the snack bar.

She grabs a handful of T-shirt and jerks me out of line. "Hey!" I say, remembering Mom's careful ironing job. "Would you quit wrinkling the shirt?"

"I don't want a drink, Big. I don't want to watch the movie either. Let's go somewhere."

The Duane in my head wants to high-five me, but I'm not so sure. "Go somewhere? Like where?" She shrugs. *You're the guy,* says Duane. *It's your call.*

"Want to walk over to Chuck E. Cheese?" I ask her. *Chuck E. Cheese?* My brother sounds disgusted. *Is that the best you can do, Jus?*

He's right. The giant puppets will be singing and little kids banging on the game machines. But aside from the state sales tax office and an out-of-business department store with blank windows, there's not a whole lot in this strip mall.

We push the door open. The giant puppets are singing, but Chuck's place is pretty empty. I change my last three dollars for quarters—Jemmie says she'll pay for our next undate—and we hit a Star Wars battle game. I know it'll cheer her up to beat me, so I let her. Or I would let her, if she wasn't winning already.

It isn't long before I run out of change. "May as well go back," she says. I feel like I let her down. I want to slink into the dark theater and disappear. Instead, Jemmie finds a bench in the lobby of the theater and pulls me down beside her. We don't say anything for a while, but her leg is touching mine. She probably hasn't noticed.

"Who is that guy with the little mustache?" she asks staring at the nearest silver screen star. "Looks like Hitler in a funny hat."

"Charlie Chaplin." It's a lousy likeness, but the mustache and derby are dead giveaways. "The guy next to him is Clark Gable."

"Who's Clark Gable?"

"You know, *Gone with the Wind?*" She shakes her head, no. "You haven't seen *Gone with the Wind?* Oh, you have to. Maybe you can come over and watch it sometime. Find out what the Civil War was really all about." Then I remember there are slaves in it and stuff like that. "Or maybe we could watch something else. Mom's got a couple starring Hitler in a funny hat," I say, pointing at Charlie Chaplin.

The movie lets out. "Jemmie, where did you go?" Cass demands as she and Ben rush over.

"Ask Big." Jemmie looks at me like we have some great secret. Even though I know she's only trying to make her friend jealous, I give her the look back.

"What?" Ben says. We both laugh. "What happened?" It's just a bluff, but it feels good to see *them* look left out. And if they're on the outside, then Jemmie and I are on the inside.

We all squeeze into a VW beetle Mr. Floyd is taking out for a test run. He makes Ben ride shotgun—probably some kind of parental control on backseat messing around since the seat is so small and it's dark now. Jemmie and I sit mashed together. I'm wondering if she minds sitting so close when something touches my leg. I look down. There's Ellie, barely visible in the dim parking lot lights, trunk raised in challenge.

We wrestle to the death, jostling Cass. Just as we pull up to my house I pin her. "Two for two," I say, and I climb over her and out.

○

I come in the house whistling. Mom pauses with a spoonful of ice cream halfway to her mouth. The open carton is balanced on her knees. I feel bad. She binges when she's lonely—like me. "How was the undate?" she asks as I fall onto the sofa beside her.

My skin still tingles where Jemmie's leg pressed against mine. "It was okay."

"Did that girl try anything?"

"You're thinking of your other son. I'm classic just-a-friend material. Classic."

She puts her hand on my arm. "If nothing happened, then why are you glowing?"

"I am *not* glowing, Mom."

"Yes you are." She tries to look into my eyes, but I slide out of her grip and disappear into the kitchen. I open the refrigerator and stick my head inside.

"You wouldn't be getting a crush on Jemmie Lewis, would you?" she calls after me.

"Can't hear you, Mom." I'm preparing to go into complete denial when the phone rings. "I got it."

"Hey, Jus." It's Duane. "How goes it?"

I lower my voice. "You're not going to believe this, Duane. That thing you said about helping girls make up their minds—it worked."

"What?"

"You know—what you said in your letter. I just had sort of a date with Jemmie Lewis. We held hands—sort of."

"Way to go, little bro! You made it to first base—sort of."

"Life isn't all baseball, Duane. It isn't. You'll get a letter I sent this morning about it—guess I could've saved a stamp..." But as I babble I realize something's wrong. "Hey, it's Friday, not Monday. Why are you calling?"

Mom's still eating ice cream—and I'm still hoping this will be a normal bullshit call. But when he speaks again I can tell it won't. "Is Dad back yet?"

"Nope. Still AWOL."

I hear him blow out, then take a deep breath. "I got my orders. I'm going OCONUS."

"What's that in English?"

"Sorry. That's off the continental U.S. I'm shipping out."

"To where?" I whisper. It seems important that Mom have another blissful minute when it's just her and the Mocha Almond Fudge.

"The guys' best guess is somewhere in the Persian Gulf—Kuwait, probably, then Iraq." I hear the spoon click as Mom sets it down on the coffee table.

"Justin? Is that your brother?" Her voice trembles so bad she sounds like an old lady.

Duane must hear her in the background. "Put Mom on."

"Be careful," I tell him.

"You know I will," he says. But I'm not talking about him going to the Gulf—I'll worry about that later. Right now I mean be careful what you say to Mom.

125

"Stay put," I tell her and I walk the cordless to her. Maybe she should be sitting when she gets the news.

As she listens to him, she closes the ice cream carton. "How soon?" she asks. "Seventy-two hours! My Lord..." She covers her eyes with her hand. "Yes, I can track down Dad."

"You can?" I say. I thought he just dropped calls on us like water balloons: he can hit us, we can't hit him.

She hangs up. After sitting with her face in her hands for a minute, she gets up slowly. I follow her into Dad's study. Penciled on the back of an envelope is a number. She carries the envelope back to the couch and punches in the numbers. Rubbing her eyes with her fingers, she listens to it ring. When someone at the other end of the line answers, she sits up perfectly straight. "Put Jack on. I need to talk to him. Now."

I know the instant she hears his voice because her lips tremble. Then she gets ahold of herself. "Hello, Jack. For your information, Duane's going. He's shipping out." She sounds businesslike. She listens for a moment, then says, "Seventy-two hours. That's all, Jack, I thought you should know." She's pulling the phone away from her ear, then she stops. "What? Yes, he's here."

In one movement, Mom hands me the phone and lies down on her side on the couch.

"Hello?"

"Jus. Are you okay?"

"Should I be?" Half an hour ago I was better than okay, I was great. That doesn't seem to matter now.

"Don't worry, Jus. Everything's going to work out. I guarantee it."

"Great, Dad. That's great." When I push the "end" button I want to vanish into Duane's room, but I can't leave Mom curled up on the couch hugging a throw pillow. I cover her with a blanket and put the Giz next to her on the couch where she can pat him if she needs to. I take up my post in Dad's recliner.

I can't handle this anymore. It's too hard.

Then I remember the last thing Dad said. *Everything's going to work out. I guarantee it.* I sit bolt upright in the chair because suddenly I know. Right now, right this second, Dad is getting in the car in Atlanta…he's turning on the ignition…he's coming home.

I wake up several times during the night thinking I hear the sound of a key in the lock. Each time I wait for the shout. *Hey, Jack is back!*

It's never anything but the creaks and clicks the house makes when it's windy.

O

Something grabs my shoulder. I let out a strangled scream. My eyes pop open. Mom is a ghost leaning over me, all ectoplasmic with the blue light of the TV behind her. The digital clock on the corner of the screen says four twenty-two; shouldn't he be here by now?

"Justin," she whispers. "Let's go up to bed." I feel about five as she helps me to my feet. Her hands on my back, we chug up the stairs like a slow freight train.

"This is my stop," I say as we pull even with Duane's door.

She doesn't try to kiss me. "Sleep tight," she says, and her fingers trail across my back.

Dear Duane,

It's 7:15 Saturday morning. I guess you're wondering what's going on. The Riggs never roll out of bed this early on a Saturday unless it's Christmas. Your call made it kind of hard to sleep. Mom's downstairs vacuuming her heart out. You know Mom. Intense vacuuming means she's either worried or pissed—it's never about housecleaning.

Remind me why you enlisted—you didn't have to do it. If you were still here the units would be fighting but Dad would be home. You'd never let things get this crazy.

BTW Mom reached Dad with your news. It's got to bring him home right? He's not here yet but hopefully soon. So I guess you're still fixing things.

I liked your old way better.

Justin

I stare at the ceiling over the bed. "Give it a rest, Mom," but the whine of the vacuum cleaner downstairs never lets up.

Lying there, I imagine Dad in different places around the house: Dad in the recliner, Dad with his elbows on the table reading the paper. Duane's news has to bring him home. But if he got in the car right after we hung up he'd be here by now. What's keeping him?

I get out of bed and pull on my pants and a shirt. I do half a chin-up. From the top of the stairs I see the snout of a vacuum cleaner attachment. It sucks the dust out from between a pair of stair rails and retreats. I lean over the banister. "Good morning, Mom."

She vacuums while I eat cereal. The sound gets fainter and louder as she drags the beast around the house. She sticks her head in the kitchen. "Help me move the couch?" We each lift an end and walk it back to the wall. She sucks up the drifts of Giz hair underneath.

I tell her to take a break, it's Saturday. But secretly I think that Dad coming home to a clean house is a good thing. I'd pitch in and help, but my own personal job is to make sure the universe doesn't suspect that I know he's coming. It could jinx the whole thing.

When I put on my sneakers the left one splits open like a gator's mouth—could be a bad sign. Trying not to think about it, I get out the old duct tape and wrap the shoe. I tape the other one too, so they'll match.

I walk around the neighborhood in my silver shoes, killing time.

When I turn the corner near my house I look, without looking, for blinding patches of white and chrome through the hedge—Dad keeps the Town Car in showroom condition. Saturdays, the two of us used to drive over Seminole Wash and Wax and ride through. Afterwards, Dad paid me five bucks to vacuum the interior while he smoked and pointed out specks of lint I'd missed.

I remember when Dad bought the car. Mom said we couldn't afford it, not when her old Corolla sounded like it was about to cough up a lung. Dad insisted. He said that for a salesman the car is crucial, replacing the Corolla could wait.

I look for the Lincoln now, but the only evidence of car I see through the hedge is the dull maroon of the Corolla, which still sounds like it's about to cough up a lung anytime Mom turns the key. What will we do when the Corolla dies for real? I could maybe get Mr. Floyd to fix it, if they still make the parts. Or Dad might have to get us another one. What does Dad owe us if he never comes back?

All of a sudden there are too many questions—too much stuff in my life I can't figure out, or change. It's not like I'm asking for a whole lot—just Dad's car in the driveway. If it were there everything would be fine, but the spot where it should be is empty, and nothing is fine.

I want to talk to someone. Not Mom; she's got enough problems. Not Ben, who's my best friend only when his girlfriend is busy. I want to talk to my undate. Duane said don't spill to a girl, but I think he meant blabbing about how you feel about her. I just want to talk about Duane and the Units...the way life sucks. That's different.

I walk toward the Lewises' house, hoping Jemmie will be on

the porch or looking out her window. When I get there—surprise—she isn't doing either of those things. I stand on the other side of the street, watching her house, stupidly hoping the situation will change.

The flag that Cass's dad mounted to the frame of the front door after September eleventh hangs limp against the house. I see he's added a bumper sticker to the wall above it: THESE COLORS DON'T RUN. That's easy for him to say. No one's going to ask an old guy like Mr. Bodine to fight.

I should leave. If Jemmie looks out she'll think I'm some kind of pervert. To buy time, I sit down on the curb and untie my shoe. I'm retying it when I hear a door open. My heart chugs up my throat, but a voice that is not Jemmie's says, "Why, Justin Riggs, how nice to see you this mornin'."

Nana Grace scuffs up to the porch rail with a cup of coffee in her hand and cranes her neck. "Just look at that sky!" she declares. "Prettiest day since the beginning of the world."

For the first time since coming out for a walk, I look up instead of down. "It's the same sky we had yesterday, isn't it? What's so special?"

"Sky's bluer today, like looking up at heaven. It's enough to make a person forget their knees hurt." She slides a hand down one of the porch swing's chains, lowering herself to the seat. "Care to sit and be sociable?"

When I'm seated beside her she gives us a little shove with her feet and we swing slowly back and forth to the creak of the chains. "So, how you been lately?" she asks.

"Fine, I guess."

"Fine, you *guess?*" She smooths her apron over her knees. Her fingers hesitate over the little flowers embroidered on the pockets.

I hear the door at Cass's house open, then close. I can't see who's going in or out because of the fence between the yards, but I hear Ben's voice. "I'm not trying to tee your dad off, I just don't agree with him."

"He's only being patriotic," Cass answers.

"Being patriotic doesn't mean going along with any old thing the government decides to do."

"Come on, Ben. Your family doesn't believe in war, period. But sometimes war is the only choice."

"Not *this* time." Ben sounds exasperated. "Anyway, your father didn't need to say all that stuff about my dad. Americans are allowed to disagree. It says so in the Constitution."

"But Ben, he didn't mean—"

"Forget it. I'll see ya later, Cass."

"Ben...Ben?" Cass calls. "We don't have to agree about everything. Ben!"

Ben strides out onto the street alone. Hands in his pockets, shoulders hunched, he walks past us, staring down.

"Looks like he could use a friend," Nana comments quietly.

"I'm not some faucet he can turn off and on."

"I s'pose you're right. But bein' right ain't the only thing."

We watch Ben until he disappears. "Duane's shipping out to the Persian Gulf," I blurt.

"Shipping out?" She twists the edge of her apron, forgetting Ben and his girl problems. "This thing with Iraq is like some runaway train. It ain't gonna stop 'til it runs smack into something. I'll be praying for him, Justin. The Lord listens."

I hear the door open behind us. It has to be Mrs. Lewis coming out—what are the odds on seeing Jemmie just because I want to? I stare at the duct tape on my shoes and get ready to tell Mrs. Lewis that I'm fine, Mom is fine, that everything is fine, fine, fine.

The toes of a pair of stuffed bunny slippers appear in the space between my sneakers. Above the bunnies are the flowered legs of pj bottoms and an oversized T-shirt—there goes my Vicky's Secret fantasy. I pan up to her eyes. "Hey, Big," says Jemmie.

"Oh, hi."

"It's a little chilly out here," says Nana Grace. "Let's all go inside and have us a cup of tea. And Jemmeal? Run up them stairs and get decent." But when Nana goes in, Jemmie slides into her place on the swing.

She wedges the toes of her slippers between the first two slats of the seat and hugs her knees. "What's up since I saw you thirteen hours ago?" She casually reaches over and makes an elephant on the seat between us.

"We got a call from Duane. He's going to Iraq."

"Oh, Big!" The elephant becomes a hand again, a hand that grabs mine and gives it a big squeeze. All of a sudden there are girl-getting possibilities to having a brother in danger—I feel like a creep for even thinking about it. *Whatever works*, says Duane.

But the hand-holding lasts about a second before she realizes what she's doing and lets go. "Is there any way I can help?" she asks.

"I don't think so. All we can do is sit around and wait to hear something."

"That's tough." She stretches her arms over her head and yawns real big. I have a feeling girls don't yawn like that in front of guys they like.

"Guess I better go get decent." The swing jounces as she jumps up.

I'm not swinging, just sitting, when Nana Grace pokes her head out the door. "Tea's ready."

Jemmie carries a tray of teacups to the dining room table. She's decent—but she still wears the bunny slippers. Her brother gets his tea in a plastic cup—just a little with lots of milk. "Here you go, Artie," she says. She fills her mother's and grandmother's, and then mine. Her own cup of tea is just like Artie's: a little tea and a lot of milk. She sneaks a peek at her mom. Mrs. Lewis is doing a crossword puzzle. Jemmie dumps a heaping spoon of sugar into her milky tea and stirs.

I add milk and sugar too. The tea still tastes like dirty water. To be polite I take a few sips. Mrs. Lewis glances up from her crossword to ask how I am. "Fine," I say. "Mom too." After a few minutes of tea drinking I leave. Jemmie and her mother are going shopping.

I don't feel any better. I mean, I told about Duane shipping out, but I still haven't talked. Not really. There isn't anyone to talk to—anywhere.

Dear Duane,

It looks like it's going to be a big crash and burn in the return-of-Dad department. I give him 'til Wednesday. After that, forget it.

Mom's cleaning frenzy is over. You could eat off the floor behind the fridge, it's so clean. Too bad we can't. The counters and table are still massively buried. The piles are so deep, it's like archaeology—if I dug through the layers, I bet I'd find things you left there from junior high.

Thanks for the last-minute good-bye call. I know Mom cried her eyes out talking to you, but she appreciated it.

Take care of yourself, okay?

Justin

Wednesday, February 19

It's Wednesday, deadline day. When I left for school Dad still wasn't home. I know the day's not over yet, but as far as I'm concerned, he's blown it.

I plod from class to class, churning. When anyone asks me a question, I give them the answer that requires the least thinking and the fewest syllables. Someone should stick a sign on me: "Caution: Contents Under Pressure."

I'm stumbling blindly to math when I hear piano music pouring out the double doors of the cafetorium. I knew there was a piano in there on the stage, but it's usually pushed back against the curtain, where it collects dust. Someone is playing it, someone who really knows how. The music reels me in and it's, like, all of a sudden I'm awake.

I ease into the room, which is haunted by the old-tomato smell of lunch spaghetti. The nearest table has a milk carton on it, bendy straw sticking out. The evidence that I'm still at school is everywhere, but I feel like I've been teleported to some mirror universe.

Up on stage, Mr. Butler is playing. His back is to me, and the cuffs of his white shirtsleeves are rolled up. The lid that covers the strings and hammers is down, as if he wanted to muffle the music, but he seems to have forgotten. He pounds the keys so hard that the jacket draped on the end of the bench slides to the floor.

What he's playing must be classical—it would never be on MTV or Dad's Country Oldies station.

I knew Butler was a piano teacher, but I never imagined he could play like this. He hammers one last thunderous chord, then stops. His foot leaves the pedal and the vibrating wall of sound vanishes. He checks his watch and heaves a sigh, then rolls his sleeves down. As he turns to reach for his jacket I slip out the door. I don't want him to know he had an audience. The guy was playing for himself.

○

After school I go straight to Jemmie's. Nana Grace has Artie on one hip; she bumps the door open with the other one. "Glad you're here," she says. "Me and Artie are coloring, and we could use a little music." They retreat into the kitchen, leaving me and Mr. Sohmer alone.

I'm a little nervous when I sit down. I'm not really good at this. I mean, I'm no Mr. Butler. The first key I hit plinks like a toy piano. But as I play a run of notes with my right hand, I forget the way Butler played—I forget everything. I hum the missing G and things begin to drift—or maybe rise is more like it.

Yeah, rise.

It's like letting a balloon go, only I'm the balloon. The higher I go, the more I see, and the more I see, the smaller it all seems: Dad and Mom, Duane, Jemmie, the war. Playing music is like the Big Nothing, only opposite.

The Big Something.

I play one of my songs through a couple of times. Then suddenly there's a new piece of melody in my head. I don't know where the new part came from, it just swings into place, like I'm building a bridge. With each new string of notes, I walk a little farther out.

I'm suspended above everything when I hear Cass's voice. "It's all right, your mom'll fix it, Jemmie." I turn toward her voice. The bench chirps. I'm back in the Lewises' living room.

"Easy, take it easy." The girls are outside, on the walk or the porch. Their practice can't be over yet. I should still have another half hour.

"You think you can make it?" Cass asks.

When Jemmie yelps "Ow!" I head for the door.

The girls are at the bottom of the porch steps, Jemmie wobbling on her left foot, one arm over Cass's shoulders.

"I got you," says Cass. "Now, we'll do it real slow, one step at a time. You ready?"

"What's wrong with you?" I ask.

Jemmie looks up. "I'm seeing how far I can hop, Big."

"So, how far can you?"

"All the way from the school."

"Hey, not bad."

"She hurt her leg," Cass murmurs, like she wants me to hear but hopes Jemmie doesn't.

Jemmie gives her a killer look. "I'm okay." But when she tries to hop up the first step she stumbles.

Cass steadies her. "Lean on me. Let's try again."

I jump from the porch to the ground. I sweep Jemmie into my arms.

"Sweep her into my arms" sounds so *Gone with the Wind*, which is what I had in mind, but actually doing it feels different than it looks. For a skinny girl, Jemmie is solid, heavy. As I heft her up I'm hit, *wham, wham,* with two scary thoughts.

First scary thought: I just picked up Jemmie Lewis—she's going to claw my eyes out.

Second scary thought: what if I drop her?

"I don't need help," says Jemmie. But she locks her arms

around my neck. As she rests against my chest. I smell her sweaty, spicy smell. Her breath hits my neck. I feel as strong as the Hulk after he bulks up and turns green.

I carry her up the front stairs and through the door that Cass holds open. Five steps into the room I lower her to the couch. Ten seconds total, and it's all over.

Nana Grace bustles into the room followed by Artie, clutching a purple crayon. "Lord!" Nana fusses, staring at the heap of granddaughter. "What happened to you, child?"

"It's her leg," says Cass. "It's been bothering her the last few times we ran." Jemmie's eyes are closed, but a tear draws a shiny dark line down her cheek. "She tried to push through it."

"Your left leg?" Nana asks. "Thought you'd been favorin' it." She rests her fingers lightly on Jemmie's shin. "That the place?"

Eyes still closed, Jemmie bites her lip and nods.

Artie kisses the spot. "All better," he says.

But Jemmie gasps when Nana props the leg up with a pillow. "Hey, be careful!" I say.

Nana goes in the kitchen and comes out, sliding a frozen gel-pack into a bag that closes with Velcro.

"Does this happen a lot?" I ask. "I mean, at my house when we need an ice pack we reach for a bag of frozen peas."

Nana says, "You run as hard as this child does, it happens." Jemmie winces as her grandmother settles the ice pack on her leg.

"Shouldn't we do something more? She's really hurting."

Nana runs a palm over Jemmie's forehead. "Just lie quiet, now."

"Maybe we should take her to the hospital for X rays," I say. "I can carry her to the car."

"No need." Nana Grace shakes a blanket out and covers Jemmie. "Her personal nurse'll be home in half an hour."

We sit around waiting for the nurse to arrive. To cheer Jemmie up, Cass does a fake-o imitation of me carrying her up the stairs. She holds out her arms, huffing and puffing—she looks sort of like Frankenstein. Pretty soon Artie's doing it too. I laugh, but I watch Jemmie, wondering if she sees what I see when she replays the scene in her head. There was no huffing and puffing, just gliding. Gliding—with background music.

Jemmie's personal nurse comes home at five. Mrs. Lewis takes one look at her daughter and her eyes narrow. "What's the matter, Jemmeal?" She can't seem to decide whether to be worried or to tell Jemmie to quit fooling around and get up off that couch.

"She hurt her leg bad," I tell her. "She can't even walk."

Mrs. Lewis frowns and flicks the blanket off her daughter. She kneels and lifts the ice pack and sets it on the floor. "Is this the spot?" she asks, touching Jemmie's shin. Jemmie nods. She flexes the knee and ankle joints, then, using her thumbs, she kneads the spot. Jemmie gasps.

Mrs. Lewis sits back on her heels and sighs. "We could get a bone scan, but it looks to me like you have a stress fracture."

Jemmie's eyes open. "How did I get a stress fracture? I didn't fall or anything."

"You've been training too hard, pounding the daylights out of your poor old tibia."

"You can fix it, can't you?" Jemmie pleads.

Mrs. Lewis takes Jemmie's hand. "Only thing that can fix it is time. You'll have to quit running a while, rest it."

"But I need to run!" Jemmie pulls away from her mother. Twisting so she faces the back of the couch, she pounds it with a fist. "I *have* to run!"

"And you will. After a few weeks' rest."

"How many weeks? I'll miss the whole season!"

Mrs. Lewis runs a hand along her daughter's arm. "There'll be other seasons." She goes upstairs to change out of her uniform like everything is settled. For her, other seasons are good enough—but not for Jemmie, who starts to cry quietly.

I want to say something to her that will help but I can't think of anything. Cass kneels beside the couch. "I'll stay with you, Jemmie. I don't want to run without you."

Jemmie whips around on the sofa. "You crazy, girl? Thanks to you and me, Monroe Middle has a reputation. Get out there and whup their butts for the both of us."

"Okay," says Cass, nodding solemnly. "For both of us."

"Seems like the end of the world," says Nana Grace. "But you'll see. God closes a door, he opens a window. Gotta be something useful you can do for a while."

"Sure." Jemmie flops onto her back and blinks up at the ceiling. "While I stay off my leg I'll find the cure for cancer."

Dear Duane,

I carried Jemmie up the stairs—she put her arms around my neck and everything. She couldn't walk because she hurt herself running. Still, it was kind of cool. I didn't drop her or anything.

Dad blew the Wednesday deadline. He didn't come home. When he called I said ehhhhhh like a game show buzzer and hung up on him. If he doesn't need us we don't need him.

You, me, and Mom would be a decent family—plus if you were here you could give me your useless girl-getting tips in person.

Meanwhile don't worry about us. I'm okay and Mom is vertical most of the time.

BTW do you know that millions of people all over the world are demonstrating against going to war? We saw them on TV shaking signs and chanting No Blood For Oil! That might slow things down.

Justin

P.S. Girls are heavier than they look.

Leroy gazes after Ben and a bunch of guys with gloves who are all headed for the softball field. "I should be on that team," he complains. He says the same thing at the start of each new sports season. Leroy can't go out for anything because he has to watch his brother. "I'm better than Lucas, better than Weller too."

Jemmie tells him to stuff it.

Leroy eyes the cane she's leaning on. "You want to make me, Granny?"

She swats him with her cane, hard. It's the first day of official track practice and Jemmie has to sit it out. She's just waiting for her grandmother to pick her up. Leroy, Clay, and I are waiting too. Nana doesn't care how many of us pile in the back of the truck as long as we keep our butts parked.

As she pulls up, I read the lettering on the door panel of the truck: *Lewis Painting, Interior/Exterior, No Job Too Small.* I've read it before but never thought about it much. The painting business probably belonged to Jemmie's dad. I bet Mrs. Lewis got the truck in the divorce. But that would be kind of weird. If he had a painting business, he'd still need the truck.

I climb in back and it hits me. He wouldn't need it if he was dead. But Mr. Lewis can't be dead. He'd be too young. He's someplace else, hanging out with his new family.

As the truck bottoms out going over the lip of the school driveway I think, but what if he is dead? I had a friend, Jake Larsen, who died in third grade. If a third grader isn't too young, nobody is.

I watch the road through a rusty hole in the truck bed. I bet I'm the only one who thinks about this stuff. I tried to talk to Ben about it a couple of times, but he freaked. Ben thinks about things like getting more speed on his fastball.

I watch the back of Jemmie's head through the window of the truck cab—Nana Grace has her isolated up front to protect her leg. Does she ever think about dying? Maybe I'll ask her. *Great way to get next to a girl,* says Duane. *Talk about death.*

I check out the guys in the back of the truck with me. Leroy is tattooing his wrist with a ballpoint. Clay is throwing crackers left over from lunch into the air and catching them in his mouth. They don't seem worried.

And suddenly I feel the wind, and everything seems faster, better. The trees on Roberts flash by. I play a quick scale on the legs of my jeans. I wish I could get to Mr. Sohmer and make something up, that would help too, but no track practice for Jemmie means no piano practice for me. Or so I think.

When we pull into the Lewises' driveway Clay, Leroy, and I pile out of the back of the truck. I open the door for Jemmie. Still seated inside, she hooks me with her cane. "You're coming with me, Big."

"What about me?" Leroy asks, crowding in.

"Not you. Just Big." She climbs out of the truck and taps his butt with the cane—she doesn't really seem to need it to walk, but she's been using it as a weapon all day. "It's time for his piano lesson."

"I need a lesson! Please?" Leroy begs. But she shakes her head. He turns to me for help. "Justin, you want me to come with you, right?"

I let Jemmie march me up the steps at cane-point like this is all beyond my control, leaving Leroy on the driveway, looking.

Inside, Nana Grace takes Artie's sweater off and then holds out a cheek. Jemmie gives her the kiss she didn't get when we were in sight of the school, then Jemmie turns to me. "Big, I'm gonna teach you how to read music."

"Okay," I joke. "Right after you cure cancer." Then I see she's serious. "Wait! No way. Ask Nana Grace, I play by ear. Nana?"

But Nana Grace just waves Artie's sweater at me. "Won't hurt you none to sight-read. Going to have to if you really wanna use that talent of yours."

"Talent? What talent? I just fool around." Jemmie prods my back with her cane, pushing me toward the piano. "No—no way," I say. "You'll mess it up!"

The cane tip hits the floor. "Mess what up?"

"My music!" I've heard Jemmie play and I don't want to play like her. She sounds the way a paint-by-the-numbers picture looks. The notes are right but they sound dead. "The stuff I play just sort of happens," I explain. "I don't want to screw it up."

"Beethoven had music in his head," says Nana Grace, folding Artie's sweater. "Duke Ellington too. They both dead and gone. Good thing their stuff's wrote down."

I never heard of Duke Ellington, but I know about Beethoven. He's way up there on the famous dead guy list, like Shakespeare. "Yeah, but I'm definitely not Beethoven."

Nana slings Artie up on a hip. "Even Beethoven wasn't Beethoven when he started out," she calls back to me as she climbs the stairs. "He was just a kid with a few tunes in his head—kind of like you."

"Can you remember the music you make up?" Jemmie asks.

"Sure," I bluff. "I mean, most of the time I can."

Jemmie strides over to Mr. Sohmer and runs a finger across the sheet music that lies open on the piano. "What if you could write it down?"

"Like that?" The music must be what she's practicing, but it doesn't mean a thing to me. "It looks like a bunch of birds on telephone wires."

"Only because you can't read it. When I get done with you, you will."

"Is that a threat?" I ask. When she glares, I take a deep breath. "I guess I could give it a try."

The words aren't out of my mouth before she's digging through the sheet music in the piano bench. She brings out a book with dingy pages and a torn cover: *E-Z Piano Pieces for Little Fingers.*

Instant regret!

Piece number one is called "The Kitty Kat." It even has words: "Kitty kat, kitty kat, fluffy white kitty kat…." It gets worse from there. "Forget it, Jemmie. I don't think I can do this without barfing. Hey, are you listening?" But she's left the room. I hear her rattling a drawer in the kitchen.

She walks back in, pulling the cap off a black Magic Marker with her teeth. "What's that for?" Cap between her teeth, she grips my right hand and starts numbering my fingers. "Hey, that tickles! And don't bother doing the other one. I already counted. I have five on that one too."

Still holding the cap in her teeth, she jams the marker back into it. She taps a little curlicue at the beginning of the music with the marker. "Today we're going to work on the treble clef. Right hand only. You have to be *way* more advanced to use both."

"What are you talking about?" I chime out a string of chords with my left hand, just to show her.

She points to the 1 printed under the first note on the page, then prods the 1 written on my thumb. I feel like I'm back in the recorder band. We played by number then too. "You play *this* with *that*," she says.

"Great. But what is *this?*" I ask, staring at the dot with a handle printed above the 1.

"It's middle C."

"Hey, no kidding! Middle C." It's like I'm meeting someone I've only talked to on the phone.

I look at the 1 under the middle C and the 1 on my thumb and strike the key. Jemmie claps. "Boy, are you easy to please," I say.

She punches me in the kidney and continues with the lesson. "Each space and line represents a different note," she says. "The spaces are the notes F, A, C, and E. They spell FACE. You can remember the notes for the lines with 'Every Girl Beats Doug Frequently.'"

"Jemmie!" says Nana Grace; she and Artie are coming down the stairs at Artie speed.

"Okay, okay. *Most* people say, 'Every Good Boy Does Fine'—but mine sounds better."

The note that follows the middle C is on the first line, with the number 3 printed under it. Whether girls are beating Doug or boys are doing fine, it's an E. I play it. "All right!" Jemmie yells.

I follow the spots across the page, pecking at the keys. It's as if there are strings between the numbers on the sheet music and the numbers on my fingers.

If I make a mistake Jemmie points it out immediately—I begin to feel like Doug (the guy girls beat frequently). By the time I strike the final middle C, sweat is trickling down my sides. It took me twenty minutes to play the E-Z piece once—"The Kitty Kat" kicked my butt.

"That was *really* entertaining," I say. "Thanks for the lesson." I launch into the tune I've been working on. It feels great. My fingers are my own again.

Jemmie jabs the first middle C in "The Kitty Kat" and looks over at me. "Again."

"Nana Grace?" I call toward the kitchen. "Make her stop!"

"You're on your own, boy," she calls back.

I struggle through "The Kitty Kat" again. The notes seem disconnected, like the parts of one of Mr. Floyd's Vehicles of Promise spread out on the ground. I crawl to the end of the piece a second time.

Tap, her finger is back on that first middle C.

"You sure that leg doesn't feel good enough to take you for a little trot around the block?" I ask her.

She sags forward, her forearms on her thighs. "I tried yesterday. I felt like I had flames shooting up my leg." She turns to me, scared. "What if I can't run anymore, Big?"

"Oh, you'll run again. Definitely. You heard your mom."

"Yeah, but when? I don't even feel like myself anymore."

I know what she means. That's exactly how I feel when I get a tune in my head and can't play it. I escape by sliding into the Big Nothing—when she can't run, she bosses people around.

"Are you going to play, or just sit there?" She stabs the first note with her finger again.

I play it again. "Not bad," she says. The corners of her mouth turn up, just a little. "I might let you live."

What she doesn't know is, having read my way through it a couple of times, I have the tune memorized. I'm back to playing by ear.

"Play it again," she says.

"Can we give it a rest?"

Maybe she's tired of hearing "The Kitty Kat," maybe she's spent enough time hanging out with Mr. Sohmer, but she agrees.

Nana gives us glasses of sweet tea. We sit on the porch,

swinging in and out of the band of light at the edge of the floorboards. "I never realized how slow everything is 'til I hurt my leg," she says. "How do you stand it? There's nothing to do. Maybe you could show me Charlie Chaplin or *Gone with the Wind*."

"Uh...I can't today." I blurt it out without thinking. It's just I feel like there's stuff I need to do to get ready. But what if that was my one chance?

"All right, I better go inside and practice myself," she says, taking the empty glass out of my hand. "I'll see ya."

You blew it, says Duane as soon as the door closes. He's right. I blew it. I just wasn't ready.

Back home the Giz greets me at the door. "What's up gizzard lizard?" I pick him up. I'm scratching his head when I notice the numbers on my fingers. "Hey, want to hear a tune?" I play "Kitty kat, kitty kat, fluffy white kitty kat" on his furry side, trying to cheer myself up. Giz gives me a warning look. "Okay, okay."

I go upstairs and take out Duane's keyboard.

Hey Bro,

Guess what? I'm learning to read music. It's a pain—but it's kind of cool too—because guess who's teaching me? Jemmie Lewis. We started this afternoon.

I'm in your room now playing the silent keyboard. As I mess around I keep getting pictures of little black dots with tails in my head. Are they the right notes? Give me a break—I only had one lesson.

So—it looks like I have a girl-getting tip for you. Write this down: to get next to a girl play piano with her. Sharing a piano bench ensures instant togetherness. (You can pay me for this tip at any time).

Justin

P.S. When the phone rings Mom and I jump. We hope it's you calling. When it isn't, we tell each other it's okay. It's not like there's even a war yet. It's just hard not knowing where you are.

Leroy shakes his head in disgust. "Piano lesson time again?" Disgust turns to begging as Jemmie propels me up the steps. "Want an audience?" he pleads. "I'll shut up and listen."

"Go check on your brother, Leroy," Jemmie tells him.

"He's okay." Begging turns to panic when we reach the top of the steps and it's clear that I'm getting inside and he isn't. He trots up the stairs and catches the edge of the closing door. "Can I call you later?"

"Bye," says Jemmie.

"All right," he says as she pulls the door shut, "I'll call you…"

Okay, so he's calling her later, but right now he's outside, dragging his sorry butt down the porch steps, and I'm inside with her. Wow. The power of music.

She wants to number my fingers again. "I have that part down," I tell her. But I let her—it's almost like holding hands. She takes the E-Z book out of the bench, flattens it open, and silently prods the first note with a finger.

"Are all E-Z pieces about cats?" I ask as I begin the second piece. "Cat and Mouse" has lots of big jumps between notes, like a cat pouncing. Each time I mess up she sends me back to note one.

I'd never let on, but being inside with Jemmie isn't as great as Leroy imagines.

About halfway through my second lesson I'm sweating, but I'm playing "Cat and Mouse" perfectly—I don't tell her that I have it memorized. She thinks my sight-reading is awesome.

She turns the page. Piece three: "The Squirrel Dance." She points. "Go ahead, Big, read this one."

"What's this part?" The set of lines she calls the treble clef has company. A second set of lines hangs below it.

"That's the bass clef. Just ignore it."

"I can do that." For a second it's birds on wires all over again. But it isn't—I'm beginning to know this stuff. The first note is my old friend middle C, which I hit with my number one thumb. The next note, which is on the first line, is an E, then there are a couple of Gs, which, of course, I have to hum because Mr. Sohmer doesn't have a G. I play C, E, hmm, hmm. C, E, hmm, hmm. Now, what's that note? I take a guess and hit an A.

"B, Big. It's a B. Start over."

I finally crawl to the end of the piece. "How about a break?"

"Again," she says. I let out a huge sigh and start, C, E, hmm, hmm, C, E, hmm, hmm. Suddenly, a key I'm nowhere near plays a low tone. I look over. Her left hand is on the keyboard. Next, we each strike a key, exactly together—it sounds perfect. But after that one perfect note I start to screw up. It takes me too long to figure out the notes. "Keep up, Big!" She slaps out the rhythm on my thigh with her free hand. I feel like I'm running. I breathe through my mouth.

Sometimes, for maybe three notes, we get it right, and it's great. When we reach the end it's me who says, "Again."

The second time around, I begin to nail "Squirrel Dance." Playing it becomes a race. We go faster and faster. I reach across her and play my part one octave below hers. Not to be outdone, her free hand jets under my arm and she plays the treble clef along with me. "Oh, yeah?" I sling my left arm around behind her and hit random notes at the booming low end of the keyboard. We get all tangled up in each other; we start to laugh.

She feels warm and heavy as she leans against me. Her hands drop into her lap. "That is the most fun I've ever had playing the piano." She sits up straight and pulls her feet up, folding into herself. Her heels hook over the edge of the bench and she rests her cheek on her knees. "About the *only* good time I've had playing this piano. Most times I sit on this bench and count the minutes. I don't get it. No one makes *you* do it and you keep coming back."

"I must be crazy, right?"

She lifts her head and looks into my eyes. "Can I show you something, Big?"

"Sure." The something is probably nothing, but my heart *ka-chunks.*

"Move your butt." She kneels on the floor. The hinges squeal as she opens the bench. What she's looking for is at the very bottom, under the rest of the sheet music: a thin notebook wrapped in a plastic bag that has been carefully taped. She bites her lip, concentrating as she peels the tape back and slides the spiral notebook out.

"What is it?"

With one hand she sweeps *E-Z Piano Pieces for Little Fingers* off to one side. She gently sets the notebook in its place and opens the cardboard cover. Instead of the blue lines of an ordinary notebook, this one has musical staffs printed on it.

"I didn't know you could buy music paper."

"You're gonna need some yourself soon."

On the yellowed paper in front of me are drawn-in notes, quick and scratchy, as if the person couldn't get them down fast enough. A middle C flashing a double tail like two quick flags is followed by an E that is tied by a bar to an F and a G.

I can almost hear it in my head. "What's that?" I ask, pointing to a symbol after a C.

"That's a sharp." She fingers the black note next to the C.

Notes hover above and below the staffs, so many notes they swarm the page. Whoever wrote this piece was overflowing with music. I can feel the excitement in the notes. "Go on— play it," I say.

"You think because I know where to find a C-sharp I can play this?"

"I thought you were going to play it for me so I'd know what I had to look forward to."

At the top of the page it says "Sweet Leona," by Marvin Lewis. I can almost hear Nana Grace saying, *Mmm-mm, Marvin, this boy got the touch.* "Who is Marvin Lewis, an uncle or something?"

"Marvin Lewis was my father."

"Was?"

"He died right before we moved to this house."

"Oh, man. I'm sorry. Why didn't you ever tell me?"

"I don't like to talk about it."

"Is this your dad's piano?"

"Uh-huh." She slides a finger along the keys, stroking the satiny ivories. "You remind me of him, the way you play. He could read and write music, but all he had to do was hear something once and he could play it."

She doesn't look at me; it seems hard for her to talk. She must have loved him a lot. I don't know what to say either, so I say the first dumb thing that comes into my head. "Did the G work back then?"

"Nana," she calls toward the kitchen. "Did the G work when Daddy got the piano?"

"Never did," Nana calls back. "He got it cheap. You remember, child. He used to sing it just like Justin does."

"I forgot." It seems to bother her that she forgot. She picks at a scab on her knee.

"Don't." I nudge her fingers away. "Who's Leona?"

She rolls her eyes. "My mother…who do you think?"

Sweet Leona? She's never seemed sweet to me, but I guess she was sweet to Jemmie's dad. Maybe she was sweeter before he died. "I sure wish I could hear this."

"Oh, you will, Big. You'll hear it."

"When?"

"When you play it."

"You're kidding, right? See any difference between this and this?" Sitting beside "Sweet Leona" is "Squirrel Dance," a tune as simple as a pile of rocks. "I'm struggling to get through the E-Z pieces. I'll never be able to play anything as hard as 'Sweet Leona'."

"Not with *that* attitude, you won't. You give up too easy." She stands abruptly. "Lesson's over."

"What?" I stand too, and before I know it I've been shoved out the door. "What's the matter, Jemmie? What did I do?"

"Bye," she says.

All of a sudden I'm Leroy, staring at the wrong side of the door. I don't get Jemmie. She's hot and she's cold. I'll never figure her out.

I get scared walking home—was that the end of the Big and Jemmie thing? Was that my last lesson? I think about her father's music. I see the scatter of notes he sketched across the page. To play it would take major league sight-reading, but maybe I could get there. Maybe. It would take a lot of lessons.

Wouldn't that just make Leroy's day.

○

When we roll up to her house on Wednesday, I climb out of the truck not knowing whether or not I have a lesson. She crooks a finger at me, "Come on," and I start breathing again.

"Oh, man...," says Leroy as I follow her inside.

Her dad's music is gone. Neither one of us mentions it; we just go back to "Squirrel Dance."

She teaches me about whole notes, half notes, quarter notes, sharps and flats—sight-reading never gets easy, but I keep at it. Even if I never get good enough to play "Sweet Leona," I want to be able to write my own stuff down.

Each day, when I get to Jemmie's we work on an E-Z piece. When she gets tired of pounding the day's lesson into me she wanders off. After that I noodle around. I'll make the E-Z piece minor or change the key from C to G or whatever—I've memorized the scales well enough to know when to hit a black key. I begin to work in a few little hesitations, a stutter step here and there. Music happens between the notes too.

I'm trying out a new rhythm for an E-Z piece called "Puppy Parade" when a voice says, "Syncopation."

"Synco-what?"

Jemmie is sitting on the staircase. I see stripes of her between the rails. "Syncopation." She stands and walks the rest of the way down, trailing her fingers along the railing. "That's what you call those little skips you keep throwing in. My dad used syncopation all the time. It sounds good."

And I almost say, "You hear that, Marvin? This boy's got syncopation." Instead, I launch into a piece of my own.

She falls onto the bench beside me. "What are you playing?"

"Just something I made up."

"What's it called?"

"I haven't decided yet." But since seeing her dad's music, at least to myself I've been calling it "Sweet Jemmie."

"It's pretty." She grabs a couple of hand weights out of the hall closet and does reps in time to my music; she's got to stay in shape until she can run again. "Speed it up, Big."

"You got it. Music to lift weights by," I say, picking up the tempo.

Dear Duane,

Dad just doesn't get it. He's run the clock out, but he still calls to "talk to the kid." I let him talk, he's good at it, but since I barely answer he runs out of conversation fast.

Speaking of calls, you owe us a couple. Monday nights, remember???

Since we don't know where you are or what you're doing we figure you could call any time. We stay home a lot.

Just in case you decide to write I carved a tunnel in the azaleas with some old clippers I found in the garage. I thought I'd make it easier for the mailman.

I don't even know if these letters are getting to you. If not, I guess you can't answer them. If they are, did I mention that we wouldn't mind a call or a letter? Anytime would be fine. Hint: sooner is better.

Jemmie's leg is healing—guess I won't get to carry her up the stairs again. She can't run yet but she can walk to school. She still carries the cane but she uses it more like a sword.

Justin

P.S. You never answered the question about Dad cheating.

W e're walking home from school. Ben and Cass are behind me. Leroy and Jemmie are a few steps ahead; He's finally figured out that he can get closer to her if he leaves the bike at home. At the moment, Leroy has Jemmie's cane. She's teaching him how to twirl it like a baton.

Their bodies move in unison, their strides match. They look like a couple of giraffes crossing the Serengeti on a National Geographic special. Both of them are tall and skinny. I keep hearing her in my head: *He's really, really, really…* How many "reallys" was it, three or four? I forget. Anyway—Leroy is some disgusting number of "reallys" cute. I'm trying to concentrate on my taped-up sneakers when Jemmie laughs.

What's he doing making her laugh? That's my specialty.

They're still laughing when we reach my house. I slide my arm into the azalea tunnel and drop the mailbox door. I feel to the back of the box. Only one thing in there today. I pull it out expecting it to be Wal-Mart flyer or credit card offer, something about saving whales. It's a letter.

I look at the handwriting and I let out a yell. Ben and Cass turn as a unit. "What?" Ben says.

"A letter from Duane," I say.

"When you write him back, tell him I say hi." He still doesn't know that Duane's been deployed—I thought Jemmie would tell Cass and Cass would tell him. But he doesn't seem to have a clue what this letter means to me. Jemmie does, but she's too busy horsing around with Leroy to notice what I have in my hand.

Fine. This isn't about them anyway, it's about Mom and me. She'll be excited. As I carry the letter into the house I decide to wait for her to open it.

To distract myself I eat a Baby Ruth, some leftover potato salad, a Popsicle. I finish off the last bite of potato salad and pick up a couple of pencils. I drum on things as I walk around the house.

The window glass makes a sharp *ting-ting* as I check the driveway for signs of the Corolla pulling in. Pencils bounced off the aquarium give back a dull *tong*. A couple of *tongs* and my goldfish, Xena, is nosing the glass, all excited. I take a brief intermission to sprinkle fish food. "Hey, Xena! Here comes the Giant Hand."

My drumroll on the refrigerator ends with the clatter of ice cubes falling from the ice machine to the tray.

I drum a little on Giz, who is sleeping in the recliner. Cats have lots of good points, but they're not very resonant—plus they scratch.

I circle back to the window, *ting, ting, ting,* and check on the condition of the driveway, which is improving. Mom is pulling up.

I tap my way along the wall to the door, open it, and lean out as the Corolla shudders and dies. Looking tired, Mom drags herself from behind the wheel. "Hey, Mom!" I bellow. "Good news."

She stands behind the open car door. "Good news?" She seems afraid to hope.

I yank the letter out of my pocket and wave it around.

The purse, which always hangs off her shoulder, as much a part of her as her arm, drops to the driveway. "A letter from Duane?"

"That's right, a letter from the one, the only, Duane Anthony Riggs. I haven't even read it. I waited for you."

Mom makes a dash for the steps and snatches it out of my hand. Then she just holds it and starts to cry.

"I'll get your purse, Mom," I mumble.

She looks like something out of a soap opera up there on the porch bawling. I take her inside and sit her on the sofa. "Go on, open it."

Just as quick as she snatched it from me, she hands it back. "No, you."

I tear the envelope and pull out a single sheet of paper—he could have written a little more, considering how long we've been waiting. I read, *"Dear Mom, Jus—and Dad?"* I show her the question mark after Dad. She raises her eyebrows.

"Dear Mom, Jus—and Dad? By the time you get this I should be on dry land—and I do mean dry—somewhere in the Persian Gulf. Right now I'm on a transport ship surrounded by water. Not much to do here but maintain our rifles, drill, stand watch, and get a tan. I've read a couple of books if you can believe that—Tom Clancy novels. Wish I had a fishing rod with me. Jus—tell Ben there are lots more stars out here than what we saw from the roof."

Mom interrupts. "The roof?"

"Just something the three of us did a long time ago."

"Something I don't want to know about, right?"

"Right." I go back to the letter. *"The sea's been kind of rough. I have a big old purple bruise on my hip from falling against a rope locker. Lots of the guys are barfing. So far so good for me.*

"Don't worry. From everything we hear this is going to be a quick one. And we're doing the right thing defending the US of A from a bunch of fruitcakes with WMDs and nerve gas. Mom—don't worry about the gas. I can put on my mask and clear and seal it in eight and a half seconds flat. I'll be as safe as tuna in a can.

"You can send letters and things to the Army P.O. Box on the return address. Mom: please send some undershirts and a pack of

crew socks—the kind you get eight pairs to a bag at Wal-Mart, plus as many cigs as you can. The PX on board charges an arm and a leg. Your son (and brother), PFC Duane."

I look up at Mom. "Mom, are you crying?"

"These are happy tears. See, I'm smiling."

"Smiles aren't supposed to be wet," I tell her. "There's a P.S. *I should be able to call soon or send e-mail. Mom—I have your work e-mail. Jus—give me Ben's so I can write you separately. (Guy stuff, Mom. Don't worry about it.)*

P.P.S. Jus—I'll be back to ride your ass before you know it, so stay cool."

Still crying, Mom gives me the big hug she wishes she could lay on Duane. I don't mind. I even hug her back.

Dear Duane,

Thanks for the <u>long</u> note. What are you doing—saving trees? Just kidding.

Mom and I are glad you're having a pleasant cruise. Maybe you can take the long way and get there after the whole thing is over.

Mom is bringing your letter to work to show Margaret. I pretty much have it memorized (because it's so short). The trees thank you, but make the next one longer, okay?

Justin

P.S. Mom read a list of things GI's need over there. That's why there's so much weird stuff in the box. Let me know when you figure out what to do with the baby wipes.

P.S. 2 Forget Ben. We hardly hang out anymore. I'll get you Jemmie's e-mail. I see her <u>a lot</u>.

I keep glancing at Jemmie as we walk to Butler's class together. When I wrote Duane I made it sound like she'd pass messages, no problem. I even made it sound like there was something going on between us. There isn't. She'd be walking with Leroy if he was in the same class.

"What's up with you, Big? You haven't said a word."

"We got a letter from Duane," I blurt out.

"Get out!" She grabs my arm and swings me around so fast my pack slips off one shoulder and smacks Trina Boyd, the local blond goddess.

"Do you mind?" Trina whines.

"Oh, get over yourself," Jemmie says, and she steers me past Trina toward the lockers. My pack *clangs* against a metal door. "What did he say? Is he okay?"

"He's on a transport ship. It's kind of like an all-expenses-paid cruise. Sounds like he's mostly working on his tan."

"Boy, that's great. Really great."

She sounds really happy I heard from him. I decide to go for it. "Listen, Jemmie, you have a computer, don't you?"

"Sure."

"Could I give Duane your e-mail address so he can send me messages?"

She tears a corner off a sheet of notebook paper and scribbles the address.

That's when I remember the kind of crap Duane writes me and realize this might be a major mistake. "Uh…I'd appreciate it if you didn't read them...or show them to anyone else. It'll be guy stuff. Possibly gross."

By the time the address is in my pocket, the hall is empty. We slide into English after the late bell. Trina Boyd whispers something in Jenny Stanley's ear. Jenny stares at us. I can tell they're putting Jemmie and me together like one plus one equals two.

I've probably just ruined Jemmie's reputation. But mine is definitely improving.

O

"Well, look who's here," says Nana Grace. She's kneeling on a piece of newspaper in the flower bed, her old straw hat on Artie's head. Artie's digging in the dirt with a spoon. "Where's that granddaughter of mine?"

"She said to tell you she stayed after to watch track practice. So, what are you doing?"

"Planting pansies." She tamps the dirt around a plant with the heel of her hand. "Ain't nothing like pansies for winter color."

The Lewises' orange cat butts my shin. I drop to one knee and give him a pat. "You want some help?"

"Got all the help I need right here." She lifts the hat. Artie grins at me. "Go on inside, Justin. Play us somethin' sweet."

I drop my pack on the end of the piano bench. "Hey," I say quietly. Mr. Sohmer's strings vibrate as I fold the piano lid back, echoing my greeting. The sun coming through the nearby window is pretty warm. I peel off my sweatshirt and stuff it in the top of the pack.

I start with a few scales to warm up my fingers. Then I remember Mr. Butler at the piano. Whatever he was playing, he didn't hold back. I play "Sweet Jemmie" the same way—loud, and strong.

"Amen!" comes Nana Grace's voice from the yard. "You play that thing, Justin Riggs!"

As I play I keep embellishing. Like the piece her father wrote for her mom, I want my song for Jemmie to have everything. So many new parts come I'm afraid that I'll lose them—I wish I *could* write them down. Which makes me think of the spiral notebook buried in the piano seat.

I can't explain what I do next, except that it doesn't start out bad. I just want to see "Sweet Leona" by Marvin Lewis again, so I open the bench and dig out the old binder. I haven't even touched the tape on the plastic bag when I hear Nana say, "Come on, Artie. That's enough for one day." Quick, before she can open the door and catch me, I lift the balled-up sweatshirt and stuff the music into the top of my pack.

○

When I finally peel the tape off, I'm in the Duane Riggs Memorial Bedroom. I slide the notebook out of its plastic sleeve and run a hand over the brown cover. I'm not supposed to have this. It belongs to Jemmie's mother. I guess I kind of stole it. But all I know is, closed up in the piano bench, Marvin Lewis's music is dead.

I flip the cover open and stare at the scattered notes. The only way to bring it back to life is for someone to play it, but it isn't going to be me, at least not for a long time. I'm still struggling with *E-Z Pieces for Little Fingers*. The thing is, if I could hear it a couple of times, I could maybe fake it.

I see the scene in my head. I start to play and out of nowhere, trumpets chime in—maybe even violins. The music swells. All of a sudden I'm wearing a tuxedo. The tails hang over the back of the bench. Hey, I don't look half bad. Hearing her father's music, Jemmie faints from gratitude. I turn just in time to catch her in my arms—and the music plays on…

○

"Mr. Butler?"

Butler looks up from the grade book on his desk, surprised to see an underachiever like me after the last bell. "Mr. Riggs? What can I do for you?"

"Can you play something for me on the piano?" I blurt out.

He rests on his elbows and presses his fingertips together. "Anything in particular?"

"This." I hold out the old composition notebook.

He hesitates a moment, then opens it on top of the grade book on his desk. "My, my. Jazz." He taps out a rhythm with his palm and hums a few notes. "Pretty complex stuff." But even as he says it he's pushing his chair back. "Let's see what we can do with it, shall we?"

I follow his polished shoes as they click down the silent hall. When we get to the cafetorium, the chairs are up on the tables. "Good afternoon, Avis," Butler says to a woman in a blue smock who's mopping the floor. "I hope you don't mind a little hot jazz while you work."

"Hot…cold…" Avis slops the mop around. "Don't make a difference to me."

Butler and I climb the steps to the stage. I stand behind him as he opens the notebook and centers it on the piano. Off comes the jacket, which he folds neatly and places on the end of the bench. He uncovers the keyboard, then sits and flexes his fingers. He puts his fingers on the keys, then takes them off to shift the music half an inch to the left.

Just when I think I'm going to scream he swoops down on

the keys with such force that I hear the handle of Avis's mop hit the floor.

I try to follow the notes on the page; it's like hanging onto the end of a whip. The piece starts out fast and happy, the notes popping out, but on the second page it slows, and the melody gets kind of—sexy.

When I turn the page for him, Butler glances up at me. I figure I must have turned at the wrong time, but then he goes on playing. After that the song turns sad, almost like Marvin Lewis knew he wasn't going to be around too long. That's the way it ends—the last few notes just fade, like he's wishing for something he knows he won't ever get.

"My goodness," says Mr. Butler. The last chord quivers in the air a moment longer, then he takes his foot off the pedal and folds his hands in his lap.

The silence is broken by enthusiastic clapping. It's Avis, giving Butler a round of applause. When neither of us responds, the clapping fades, and I hear the sound of water falling in the bucket.

Butler turns and looks over his shoulder at me. "That was really something, wasn't it?"

"Yeah. It sure was."

"You read music," he says.

"Not really."

"You knew exactly when to turn the page."

"It was sort of a lucky guess. I mess around on my neighbor's piano."

He stands and sweeps his jacket off the end of the bench. "Sit. Play me something."

"No, really, I can't. I'm not any good."

"Oh, come on," says the cleaning lady, leaning on her mop. "You're among friends."

I can feel "Sweet Jemmie" in my fingers. Like Mr. Lewis's

piece, it wants to be played, but I'd just screw up. "No...really." I fall back a couple of steps. Mr. Butler grabs my arm.

"Whoa! One more step and you'll fall off the stage." He lets go. "Some other time, perhaps." He closes the cover of the composition book and hands it to me. "This Marvin Lewis writes beautiful music."

"Yeah. Thanks for playing it for me. I gotta go." I jump down off the stage.

"Mr. Riggs?" I look up at him. He's just a dumpy guy in a wrinkled suit again. The music that's in him doesn't show at all. "I know you didn't come in for an English consultation, but your grade has been sliding. You used to be a good student. What happened? You don't seem to be taking it seriously anymore."

"It's not English, Mr. Butler. It's not you either. It's just...I have a lot of other stuff on my mind."

"I'm afraid that's no excuse—"

"I'll see what I can do." I glance over at the door.

"You know," he says, following me down the steps, "whenever I'm worried, I turn to my music. If you think the piano would help, have your mother give me a call." He slides a card out of his wallet and hands it to me. "I give lessons."

I learn from the card that Butler's full name is Percival Marcus Butler. With a name like that it's a miracle he lived past early childhood.

Halfway down the hall I drop the card in the trash. I almost go back and fish it out again. I'd like to learn how to play better, but music is the first thing I've ever felt like I'm good at. What if Butler told me that I'm not?

○

It's weird how fate sometimes gangs up on you. Mom is barely through the door when she says, "I ran into Jemmie's grandmother at Publix. She tells me you've been playing the piano at their house."

"Yeah, sometimes."

"Why didn't you tell me about it?"

"It's nothing, Mom. I mess around, pick out a few tunes."

"She says you have a natural ear for music, a real gift. You know, I always thought you did. You were such a singer when you were little." Mom rummages through her purse. "She gave me the name of someone from the school who teaches piano lessons. Here it is…a Mr. Butler?" She glances up from the scrawled-on grocery receipt. "I think he teaches English."

"Mega-butt Butler. I have him second period every day."

"Would you like to take lessons?" Her eyes sparkle. She wants to do something nice for me. She knows things have been rough.

"I'll pass on the lessons. But could we get a piano? They have them at Goodwill sometimes for, like, a hundred bucks."

"A piano?"

"You know, eighty-eight keys, some black, some white. We could put it in my room."

"There isn't any room in your room."

"There is if we get rid of the desk. I can sit on the bed to play."

She lays the receipt on the table and smooths it with her fingers. "I'd have to ask your father."

"Why, Mom? We don't need his permission!"

"I don't make enough to just buy a piano—even a hundred-dollar piano. We'd have to ask him for the money."

"Forget it, just forget it." I sweep the piece of paper up and crush it. For the second time in an hour I throw Mr. Butler's number in the trash.

Dear Duane,

You probably don't get CNN out there. If not, here's a flash: Saddam has forty-eight hours to vacate Iraq. It's like, "Come out of that country with your hands up." If he doesn't, the war starts.

Remember that stupid joke you used to tell about when the hit fits the shan? It looks like it's about to happen. The hit is about to fit the shan—big time.

Survival instructions from your old pal Mr. Barnett: Don't be a hero.

Survival instructions from me: The day they decide to send you into the war, get fake-sick—you're the master.

Justin

WEDNESDAY, MARCH 19

It's been about a month since Duane shipped out. I've played a lot of piano (real and silent); plastic recorder too. Music must use the same part of the brain as worrying.

Since I can't play music when I'm at school, I worry. Today I'm walking around Monroe Middle feeling like Wile E. Coyote. Now what the heck is that? wonders the about-to-be-clobbered coyote as he listens to the whistling sound of the falling anvil Road Runner just pushed off the cliff.

The difference is I know the anvil is falling. I just can't get out of the way. Saddam's forty-eight hours run out at eight tonight. The war is going to start.

I seem to be the only one who knows about it. It's a normal day at school. So it's probably completely random when Butler assigns us an essay that begins: If I could change the world...

What would I change, Mr. Butler? Plenty. There'd be no fighting. No parents arguing, no wars. In my world there'd be no tragedy called *Romeo and Juliet*. The Capulets and Montagues would work things out around the old backyard barbecue grill while scarfing down hot dogs and baked beans.

Fixing the world is the only thing I do all day that takes my mind off the war. Somehow I make it to the last bell. Jemmie sticks around for track practice again, even though it just depresses her.

Soon I'll be at her house, playing the piano, not worrying.

○

I worry plenty walking to the Lewises'. I beam psychic messages to the other side of the world. *I need to hear from you, Duane, I really need to hear from you.* I stop at my mailbox and plunge a hand in. I come up with a credit card offer. It goes straight into the garbage. Suddenly I remember that his last letter said he might call.

And I get this gut feeling that he will. Instead of heading straight for Jemmie's, I go in and check the answering machine. No messages. Zippo.

But what if he calls in half an hour? I'd kill myself if I got back from the Lewises' and the light on the answering machine was blinking: "It's me, Duane. Hi, Mom. Jus, buddy? Be cool. Call you when the war is over." He'd probably leave me one last girl-getting tip to remember him by.

I call Nana Grace to tell her I'm not coming. I hang up fast. What if he called during the one minute I was on the phone?

Maybe Saddam surrendered while I was at school. I turn on the TV. If he has, no one mentions it.

I feed Xena. Then I sprint up and down the stairs. Duane used to do that when it was too rainy to run outside. He was building lung capacity; I'm trying to prevent spontaneous combustion.

When I hear a car door slam, I run to the porch. Mom is doing her own sprint up the steps. "Anything from Duane?" she asks. She must be beaming messages to the other side of the world too. I shake my head no, but she brushes past.

When I catch up to her in the kitchen she is staring at the unblinking red light on the answering machine.

○

It's almost ten o'clock when the war begins. The first barrage of Baghdad doesn't last long. A few bombs explode over the city. Antiaircraft fire crackles from the ground, lighting up the smoky air. It is already tomorrow morning in Iraq; the sun's about to rise. In the dim light, traffic begins to fill city streets.

"They need to get inside!" says Mom. "My goodness, you don't think they're going to work, do you?"

"Maybe," I say, watching the start of a rush hour halfway around the world. "It's the little things that make life seem normal, remember?"

O

I turn the tube on as soon as I get home the next day. A lot could have happened while I was wasting time at school. The bombing seems to have picked up. "Look at that, Giz." Trenches filled with oil are in flames, set ablaze by the Iraqis. Columns of smoke flicker with lights as stuff explodes. It's eerie and, in a strange way, kind of pretty.

In all the time I watch, the cameras never show a single human, alive or dead. It's all smoke and *ka-boom,* about as real as a video game.

Mom comes home. She sits down on the couch and knots her hands in her lap. "What's happening?"

"More Fourth of July." She winces at a series of dull thuds from the TV. I try to reassure her. "Duane isn't part of it, Mom. They're saving the ground war for later. These guys are Air Force. They'll probably blow the place up before Duane has to do a thing."

"You're sure Duane isn't in the middle of this?"

"Positive." I sound way more definite than I feel. Who knows? Maybe the Air Force heard there was this genius

Army mechanic named Duane Anthony Riggs and they borrowed him. "He's fine."

"He's fine," she echoes. She stands quickly like she's glad *that's* taken care of—on to the next thing. "Are you hungry, Justin? Would you like some supper?"

"I'm not really hungry."

"Then we'll think about dinner later, okay?" She walks briskly up the stairs to her room as if "collapse on bed" is the next thing on her "to do" list. She closes her door.

She'll bury herself under the covers and fall into the Big Nothing. I'm supposed to stop her, Duane would. But I don't. I think she has the right idea; I want to fall in too.

Explosions crackle on the TV—people are probably getting hurt. If I had a piano I'd disappear into the music. I wish I could go over to the Lewises' and play, but by now Mrs. Lewis is home. I watch a few more flashes on the screen.

"I'm going out a while, Mom," I shout up the stairs. I head for the only other place I can think of.

O

"Is this a girlfriend-free zone?" I ask when Ben opens the door.

"All clear," he says. "But you still might not want to come in. It's pretty grim." I hear the rattle of explosions from the next room.

"The war's on at my house too." Ben steps back and I go in. "Your mom must be a mess." Mrs. Floyd would rather brush a mosquito off her arm than squash it.

"Yeah," Ben says. "But Dad's worse. He feels responsible."

"For the war?"

"For sending guys to the war." He leads me into the living room. "Hey, look who's here!"

179

Mrs. Floyd manages a quick hi before turning back to the TV. Mr. Floyd waves in my general direction. He never takes his eyes off the writing pad balanced on the arm of the sofa.

"Hey, Justin," calls Ben's little brother, Cody. "Watch this!" He tosses a ball in the air and tries to catch it in a cup. He misses and tries again. Even when Cody's ball bounces off his head, Mr. Floyd barely glances up from his writing.

I look over his shoulder. Ben's dad is compiling a list of names. "Hey, I know some of these guys. Didn't they used to live in your backyard?"

"Sure did. Now every one of them is in some branch of the military."

"Bobby Grimes," I read. "I remember him."

Mr. Floyd taps the name with the pencil point. "Smart kid, no money for college. He lived with his aunt. I told them the Air Force had plenty of college money."

Ben rests his arms on the back of the couch. "Hugh Cox. We remember Hugh, don't we, Jus?"

"Not the brightest kid in the world," Mr. Floyd says. "But he was good with his hands."

"Good with his hands!" Ben snorts, and we both bust out laughing.

"He was," says Mr. Floyd. "What's so funny?" He smiles as if he wants in on the joke.

"One time, while you were inside, he ground Justin's face in the dirt, Dad. He did stuff like that all the time."

Ben's mom takes her eyes off the screen. "Why didn't you boys tell us?"

"Guys don't tell," says Ben.

"That's right," I say. Come to think of it, it was Hugh Cox who told us that.

Ben and I trade looks—Hugh Cox getting shot at is not necessarily a bad thing. And all of a sudden, Ben and I are okay with each other.

Mr. Floyd's pencil point settles on another name. "Duane Riggs. Your brother's still in training, right? At least he's safe for now."

"Uh…Duane shipped out a while ago. He's somewhere in the Gulf." I glance at Ben. He's stunned. Why didn't I tell him about my brother? For a second I wonder myself. Why didn't I? Then I remember all the time he hasn't spent with me lately. If he doesn't know, it's his own fault.

Cody scoots over. "Sit next by me, Justin." I sit by the kid. Ben throws himself into a distant chair, his back toward me. I stay for, like, twenty minutes. Then I say, "Guess I better go. Mom's making supper."

I'm barely out the door when Ben shoves me from behind. "Thanks for telling me about Duane."

I whip around and shove him back. "Why should I tell you?"

"Why?" He sounds hurt and confused.

"You didn't seem interested." The street lamp throws our shadows out ahead of us. His stands still as mine walks away. Some friend. He's going to let me go. Suddenly the shadow darts across the pavement. A hand grabs my arm.

"What are you talking about?" He spins me around. "Of course I'm interested!" He puts his hands on his hips, jamming his thumbs into his front pockets. His chin juts out. That's the way Duane stands when he's mad. Standing like that, Ben looks more like my brother than I do—same brown hair and everything. And I remember Duane and Ben in the street, lobbing a softball back and forth, winging it half the length of the block. Duane was a big brother to Ben too; we shared him.

"I guess I should've told you," I admit.

"Damned straight you should've." He's breathing hard. If there was enough light I'd see his pulse twitching in his neck. "I'm supposed to be your best friend."

"Yeah? Well you might try acting like it."

His hair falls over his eyes as he stares at the ground. When he looks at me again, I can see he's not mad anymore; he's embarrassed. "This boyfriend-girlfriend thing? It takes up a lot more time than I thought. It's a lot of work."

"*Work!* I've seen you with Cass. You're loving every minute. I gotta go."

He steps in front of me and puts his hands on my shoulders. "Come on, tell me about Duane."

"What's there to tell? He shipped out. We got one letter from him."

"Yeah, I remember when you got it. What did the letter say?"

"He was on a transport ship. He said the other guys were barfing, but he was okay. He was getting a tan. Oh yeah, he said to tell you that there were way more stars at sea than we saw the time we camped on the roof."

Ben turns and we start walking together; his stride falls in with mine. "Your folks ever find out about that night?"

"Nah." As we walk between street lamps a comfortable dark settles around us.

"That was really great, wasn't it?" he asks.

"Primo." The great roof campout happened a couple of summers ago. Dad took a trip to Destin and for once invited Mom along. Of course Ben stayed over—we didn't tell his parents that Duane was in charge. We piled snacks behind the chimney. We lay on our backs and watched satellites pass over.

"We should do that again sometime," Ben says as we round the corner by my house.

"Yeah. Like that'll happen. You're on boyfriend duty 24-7."

"No, really. Just name the night," he says, and he walks me up the path to my house.

"You got time to come in?"

He stops at the foot of the steps. "I better get home. See ya." As he takes off he yells, "I'm not with her 24-7!" He vanishes behind the hedge.

"Excuse my mistake," I yell back. "Make that 28-9!" His fist appears over the top of the bushes, one finger sticking up— and he's not making an elephant.

"Same to you!" I shout. I can feel myself smiling. I know he's smiling too. I go inside trying to think of a way to ask Mom if we can camp on the roof, but Mom is still in bed.

Suddenly, I'm really, really hungry. Supper's not going to happen unless I make it. I put eggs in a pot: two for me, two for Mom. As I run water over them, the thud and pop of exploding artillery on TV sounds like fireworks in the street. I pretend it's last summer and Ben and I are setting them off.

Dear Duane,

I hope the war gets over quick. Watching it on TV is really getting to us. To avoid it Mom went straight to bed after work—she did not pass go, she did not collect two hundred dollars—and she _definitely_ didn't make supper. And what did I do? Some major eating of course. I made myself an egg salad sandwich with four eggs—and you know I don't even _like_ eggs. The sandwich was so humongous I could barely get my mouth around it. Still I engulfed the whole thing. Surprise! It didn't help.

The only thing that helps at all is walking away from the TV. I'm in your room now—disgustingly full of eggs. Mom's up again, glued to the tube. I guess I'll work on a few tunes on the silent keyboard. Mom's got the war covered. She'll let me know if anything goes really really wrong.

Stay safe.
Justin

Mom wakes me up before the alarm goes off. "Justin?" she whispers. The skin under her eyes looks bruised, like two dark thumbprints. "It's happened!"

"What's happened?"

"The first casualties. A helicopter crash."

I shoot straight up in bed. "Duane, Mom? Was Duane on it?"

"No, they were Marines and British Commandos. Sixteen killed. Every one of them is someone's kid."

I shock Mom with a big wet kiss on the cheek. I feel bad for those sixteen dead kids, their parents too, but it isn't Duane. To me Duane not being dead is the main thing. I whistle as I get dressed for school—but quit when I realize what I'm doing. Sixteen dead is a lot.

O

At my house, we fall asleep with the war, we wake up with the war. At school it gets a one-second mention on the morning announcements: "Please think of our troops overseas as we stand and say the pledge." Then we slap our hands over our hearts.

After the pledge, seventh-grader Kent Brandt recites the lunch menu: tacos with fiesta corn and beans and milk or choice of assorted beverages. I tap out the rhythm of the menu on the edge of my desk. I could make better use of the time. Second period, Butler expects me to turn in an essay on "My

Hopes and Aspirations." I haven't even started. Then there's the algebra test coming up tomorrow. I'll flunk it for sure—but does it matter?

In the hall I wait for someone to say something about the war, but the big buzz is Jenny Stanley's short haircut. She hasn't cut her hair since, like, the first grade. The girls are taking a survey. *What do you think of Jenny's hair?* The war gets one mention in the morning announcements—after that it's all about Jenny Stanley's hair.

I make it through first period health class without actually hearing a word, then do the zombie walk to English.

My knee jitters against the leg of my desk. Mr. Butler, oblivious to the fact that bombs are falling, claps his hands. "Pass your hopes and aspirations forward, people!" Papers rustle. Butler doesn't seem to notice that I don't add anything to the pile. He consolidates the stacks from the five rows and taps them on the edge of the desk. "Get out your books for silent reading."

I hold the open book in front of my eyes. Every now and then I turn a page to make it look realistic.

The bell rings. As I push the chair back Butler says, "Mr. Riggs? Please stop by at the end of the day today."

"Uh...okay." I could make up some lame excuse, but I'm too tired. I trudge to algebra, which will be followed by tacos and that pre-digested barf the school menu calls fiesta corn and beans.

○

I get all the way to his desk and stop. Butler is hunched over a page of hopes and aspirations: Jenny's—I recognize her loopy handwriting.

"So, what do *you* think about Jenny's hair?" I ask.

He looks up, confused. "Jenny's hair? Oh yes, the haircut." He clicks the point of his red pen in and out. "I'm more interested in what goes on *inside* my students' heads. Or *doesn't* go on. Sit down." He waits until I pull up a chair, then he laces his fingers and leans forward. "Mr. Riggs, are you trying to fail this class?"

I shrug. He mimics the motion, making it bigger and dumber. "What am I to think? You don't pay attention, you didn't turn in your assignment."

He acts like I'm the first kid who's ever blown off a Butler assignment. "I'll get it to you tomorrow."

"Everyone else managed to turn it in on time."

I raise my arms and let them fall to my sides. "No offense, but I don't give a crap about English right now."

His mouth opens in a startled O; his pink cheeks look slapped.

"My dad split a few weeks ago and my GI brother's in the Gulf getting shot at. I have a few other things on my mind."

"I see." Butler taps his pen against his lips. "I wish you had told me." *Tap tap tap.* His eyes widen. "But then, I think maybe you did in that composition about changing the world. I'm sorry. I should have paid more attention."

After telling Butler I don't give a crap about English I expect to get detention. Instead, he's apologizing to me.

Tap tap tap. "You know," he says, dropping the pen on the desk. "You mentioned playing the piano. When things are going badly for me, I sit down on that bench and I play like there's no tomorrow."

"I do too." I cross my arms tight. I feel like I have to hold myself together. "At least, when I can get to one."

"What is it you play, when you're able to get to a piano?"

"Things." I stare over his head at the bulletin board behind him, wondering how I got into this conversation. "Stuff I make up, mostly."

"Would you play me one of them? I'd like to hear."

"They're not really good…"

"Play for me anyway." He stands and bows toward the door. I follow him into the hall.

Each step of the way I give myself an out. If I see anyone I know, I won't do it. But there's no one in the hall.

If there's anyone in the classrooms near the cafetorium, I won't do it. But the rooms are empty.

If Avis the cleaning lady is washing the floor, forget it, I won't play.

When we get there, big wet semicircles pattern the floor. Avis and her mop have been and gone. He ushers me up the steps to the stage.

"Like I said, I'm not any good." I sit down on the bench and strike a C with my right thumb. "In fact, I stink out loud. But you'll know that in a second." I start playing "Sweet Jemmie" but my fingers feel thick and slow. I'm glad the lid is down, keeping the sound small. What I'm playing is baby music, not much better than E-Z Pieces for little fingers. What ever made me think it was good?

"Again," he says when I reach the end.

I have to forget that Butler is listening, quit smelling the clove candy on his breath and climb into the music. This time I think of Jemmie and add a hesitation here, a quick jab there. Got to show a little attitude; Jemmie's all about attitude.

"Again," says Mr. Butler when I reach the end for the second time, but he didn't need to, because now it's like I'm running down a hill with my arms wide open. The little side melodies that have appeared and disappeared over the days

I've been playing wander in and out. The final part of the tune is one I've never heard before. It does exactly what Marvin Lewis's music did: it slows and quiets and breaks off sad.

I take my hands off the keyboard, confused. I didn't expect it to end like that. I rub my palms on the knees of my jeans. "That's it, I guess."

Mr. Butler claps. "That is *exactly* it, Mr. Riggs. Grace Cunningham is right. You do have talent."

It takes me a second to realize that Grace Cunningham is Nana Grace. I can't get past the word "talent."

"Slide over," he says. Given the size of our butts, it's a one-butt bench. We sit crushed together, but he's so excited he doesn't notice. "Try holding your wrists like this. Your arm should be a single line from the elbow to the back of the hand. If you break the wrist you lose power." He attacks the keys, releasing a barrage of notes. "Like that. Now you try."

But I can't. My hands feel stupid. My palms are sweaty again.

Butler sucks in his lower lip and stares at the dusty curtain at the back of the stage. "Mr. Riggs," he finally begins. "Justin. You have a talent. Talent isn't common—but it's not uncommon either. What *is* uncommon is the will to do the work necessary to use a talent."

"But it isn't work," I blurt out, my voice shaking. "I'd rather play than do anything."

He smiles, as if he knows something I don't. "Believe me, there will be days when it will be the hardest work you've ever done." His palms land with a little slap on his thighs. "But there's nothing wrong with work." He takes another card out of his wallet and tips it against the black keys. "And don't throw this one in the trash. If your mother doesn't want to pay for lessons, we'll work something out. Okay?"

"Yeah, okay." I pick the card up. This time I stuff it deep into my pocket. "I'll think about it. I would like to...." I retreat down the steps. "Thanks. I'll see ya tomorrow."

"And when you do, you'd better have a three-page essay on your hopes and aspirations to turn in."

"Three?" I stop just inside the door. "I thought it was two."

"You're a day late...and you're still in danger of flunking English."

I step out the door, but then stick my head back in. "I'll write three pages about my hopes and aspirations, but I think you just heard them."

He bows his head in a deep nod. "Yes. I did. Sadly, I also need it in words."

As I walk away, he begins to play. I stop and lean against the wall and listen. I want to play like that.

I'm going to play like that.

O

I go out of my way to walk by Jemmie's house. If she's around, I might talk to her about Butler. I might have to mention that he thinks I have talent.

When I get close I see Jemmie on the porch swing, but she isn't alone. Leroy sits at the opposite end. Even at a distance I can tell they're not touching, but they look serious. I turn away before they spot me. Walking home, I feel as hollow as an empty soda can tossed by the side of the road.

The Corolla rolls in just as I stumble up the driveway. I paste on a smile.

Mom climbs out. Her lips brush my cheek in an automatic kiss. "Some people are saying the helicopter that crashed was brought down by friendly fire."

"Friendly fire? That means our guys were taken out by our guys, right?"

Mom nods.

"What a stupid thing to call it!" I rant. "'Friendly' is like fuzzy kittens and Mr. Rogers's sweater." I must sound pretty angry; Mom gets the worried look. "At least Duane's okay," I add, trying to calm down.

I escape to my brother's room and throw myself on his bed. Pretending it's Leroy's face, I bury a fist in the pillow. I pound it a few times but I can't keep the anger going.

Why shouldn't Leroy like Jemmie? Why shouldn't she like him?

I roll onto my back and stare up at the WWII bombers Duane and Dad built. One of them hangs silent above me like it's just dropped its payload. I make an exploding bomb sound.

"And it's a direct hit. Justin Riggs is brought down by friendly fire."

Dear Pvt. Riggs,

Take a break from saving the world. Call us or write or tie a note to a pigeon. Better yet, walk in the door. I need to ask you some questions. In case you get this letter here they are:

1. Is liking a girl supposed to make you feel like complete crap?

2. What do you do when you and another guy like the same girl only he's tall and zit free?

3. And he's your friend.

Note: Don't say pick out another girl. It's not like settling for your second favorite flavor of ice cream when they're out of the one you really want.

That's it for now. As you can see, life is good here. Take care of yourself. Don't get shot or anything.

Justin

P.S. Send answers by snail mail—don't e-mail them to Jemmie!

MONDAY, MARCH 24

Mom stands in the door of Duane's room. "How many times are you going to hit that snooze alarm? Better get up. You'll be late for school."

I roll away from her. "I can't go today, Mom. I feel lousy."

The mattress gives as she sits down on the edge of the bed. "School is important, Justin. How sick are you?"

I fake a cough so bogus my brother would be embarrassed for me. "I'm not really sick," I admit. "Please, Mom…I let you skip work right after Dad bailed, remember?"

But Mom is all bustle. "You'll feel better when you have some breakfast in you."

"I don't need food," I call after her. "I need to stay home."

"Get dressed, or go to school in your pajamas."

I put on clothes and walk downstairs. Milk and cereal wait on the table. Mom's setting out bowls when someone bangs on the front door. "Who could that be?" She pulls the sides of her robe together. "Would you get it, Jus?"

Bang, bang, bang. Whoever it is, they sound pretty anxious.

Maybe it's the end of the world. School would be cancelled for that, wouldn't it?

While Mom hides in the kitchen I open the front door. Half of the reason I don't want to go to school is standing there bouncing impatiently. "Get out here, Big." She whips the glass door open and grabs my arm. "We need to talk."

I shake off her hand. "Okay! I'm out here." I look for Leroy skulking around the area, but it's just her.

"Duane e-mailed me."

Now I grab *her* arm. "He did?"

"I went on AOL this morning and there was a message. I printed it for you." She has a piece of paper in her hand, but when I reach for it she hides it behind her back. "Listen—something happened while he was writing the message."

"Like what?"

"I don't know, but it might be bad. That's why I brought it—"

"Give it." I twist her arm, I'm in such a hurry to see what Duane wrote.

She rubs her wrist, but she doesn't complain. "You might want to sit." I'm already reading as she pushes me down on the top step:

Γrom: PFCRiggs22:

    Hey, Jemmie. This is Duane Riggs. Can you pass this message on to Justin for me? Thanks.

Dear Jus—

    I got a couple (make that five) of your letters today. Sounds like you and Mom are having a rough time. Hang in there, you'll be okay. You guys are tougher than you think.

    I can't tell you where I am but it's hotter than T Town in August. Every time the wind blows I get sand in my teeth. The important thing is I'm not anywhere near the action. In fact its kind of boring. All we do is

    Holy shit!!! Sounds like something big just blew. There go the sirens. More later. Gotta scramble...

The paper slips from my fingers. I rest my forearms on my thighs. I want to put my head down and hug my knees.

"You forgot your shoes, Justin." I look up, and there's Cass. She glances back and forth between me and Jemmie. "Is something wrong, you guys?"

Jemmie picks up the paper. "You want to show this to your mom, Big?"

"Why don't I just shoot her? It'd be quicker." I slip back in the house but only stay long enough to put on my shoes and grab my pack. "See you tonight," I yell at Mom.

"Wait, you didn't eat. Justin?"

"Gotta go. Everyone's waiting." When I get back out, Ben is there, Leroy and Clay too. They're all huddled around the printout.

"Oh, man," says Leroy. "This looks ba-ad." Jemmie slaps him on the arm. "All I said was—" She slaps him again.

The others lose interest but Ben still holds the printout. He reads and rereads it. He's as white as the paper. I should have told him about Duane being deployed right when I found out. I wish I had.

Jemmie snatches the message out of his hands and sticks it in her notebook. "We don't know anything for sure. He's probably fine." We walk to school in a clump. Jemmie and Ben flank me, like bodyguards.

○

The heat is brutal where Duane is. Things are blowing up, sirens are blaring. Here at Monroe Middle the air is cool. There isn't a cloud in the sky. It's first period, PE, and we're outside, playing a coed game of softball.

"Four to three," mutters Leroy as we stand around, waiting for our at bats. "That ain't nothin'. We can pick up a couple runs easy." But the count is two outs, no one on, and Mark Knight is up. "Just ding it, Mark," Leroy begs. "All you got to do is get on. I'll bring you home!" He rubs dirt into his palms.

The rest of the Reds look bored. Mark never gets a hit. The first pitch isn't halfway to the plate before he swings and misses. Strike one.

In the field, Ben is on the mound for the Blues. Clay is playing shortstop, Jemmie is catching. Coach told her she could sit it out because of the leg, but she hates sitting out. She told him that the stress fracture only hurts if she runs.

Leroy picks up a bat. "You're lucky, Lard." He whips the bat so hard it whistles. "Wish my brother was over there."

"What's the matter with you? You want your seven-year-old brother to get blown up?"

"Keep your eyes open, Knight!" Leroy shouts when Mark whiffs a second pitch. "No," he says quietly. "The thing is, soon as Duane gets in trouble, Jemmie is all, like, oh poor Justin. Every time I start to get close something comes up with you. Duane has a problem or you need a piano lesson. You're messing up my moves. "

"I bleed for you, Leroy."

"Just cut it out, okay? Quit being so high maintenance."

I look over at her, sitting on her heels. She smacks the glove with her fist, telling Ben it's time to put Mark Knight away. I'm not sure she thinks about either of us much.

Ben winds up and throws. It isn't even in the strike zone, but Mark wouldn't know that. He closes his eyes when the ball leaves the pitcher's hand. He swings blind...and somehow connects. The ball dribbles off the bat tip. "Run!" Leroy yells. Jemmie dives for it. It rolls over the top of her glove. Mark beats the toss to first.

"Lucky SOB," Clay shouts.

"Language, Mr. Carmichael," growls Coach.

Leroy points the bat at the sky. "Thank you, Jesus!" He swings the bat in big, cutting strokes as he walks to the plate, but stops short. He picks up a foot and taps his sneaker with the bat like he's knocking dirt out of cleats. He does the same to the other shoe.

Jemmie lifts her catcher's mask. "Sometime today..." But

Leroy has a whole routine. First he sets his feet, shifting his weight as if he's repositioning the planet at a better angle. Before raising his bat he spits in the dirt, *p-tooo.*

"You mind keeping that spit in your mouth?" Jemmie asks. If he's trying to impress her he's going about it all wrong.

"Bring it," Leroy taunts, waving the bat like a mad stinger.

And Ben brings it, tight and inside and so fast that Leroy has to suck it in and jump back. "You blind?" mutters Leroy when Coach calls a strike.

Coach thumbs his cap back. "Say something, Mr. Gibbs?"

Jemmie stands and shags the ball back to Ben. "You can play or you can whine."

"Just watch what happens to the next one," he tells her. "Ya ready now? Don't blink." But the next pitch is so far out, Leroy rests the bat on his shoulder and watches it go by. Jemmie scrambles to her feet and chases it. "Move it, Knight!" Leroy yells, and Mark Knight steals second.

On the next pitch, Leroy smacks a line drive straight at Ben, clipping him on the thigh. The bat hits the ground. *Clang.* While Ben hobbles after the ball, Leroy slides into first.

That's when Mark decides to break for third. Leroy yells. "Get your ass back on second!" Coach will give him detention for "use of language," but Leroy doesn't give a crap. Ben fires the ball to third, making Mark a sure out.

But as the ball leaves Ben's hand, Mark wheels and darts back the way he came. He throws himself down and slides. The third baseman, Angie Martinez, pegs the ball to second. When the dust settles, Mark is hugging the bag. "Safe!" yells Coach, sweeping his arms wide.

The Reds cheer. Jemmie lifts her mask. "You're up, Big."

Leroy leans so far forward his knuckles brush the ground. "Bring us home, Lard!"

I pick up the warm metal bat and wrap my hands around

it. A breeze is blowing in from right field. Ben lifts his hat. His hair is sweated to his face. The breeze feels good, I bet. He flaps his hat once like he's airing it out, and I step up to the plate.

"Come on, Big. Focus," Jemmie whispers. "You can do it."

"You're on the other side," I remind her.

While I set my feet, my best friend waits, the ball in his fingertips. I raise the aluminum bat off my shoulder, take a couple of strokes at the air, and nod.

"Got the man at the plate," chants Leroy. "*Meeeean* Justin Riggs. He shows no mercy." He raises a fist and bellows, "Jam it, Lard!"

Mark takes up the chant on second. "Jam it, Lard!" In a heartbeat all the Reds are chanting, "Jam it! Jam it!"

At my back a voice says, "Ben's a little wild, Big. You might get a walk. Otherwise you gotta hit it long."

Ben's first pitch is a grapefruit, a gimme. It's like he wants me to hit it. I don't even swing.

"Stee-rike one," says Coach. Leroy paws the dirt in disgust.

"Swing it, Big," says Jemmie tugging at my pant leg. "Don't go down looking."

I turn on her. "I'll swing when he throws me a real pitch. This is humiliating."

Jemmie slams a fist into her mitt and nods.

Ben aims the next one right at my head and hurls it as hard as he can. The ball is a guided missile and I'm the target. I jettison the bat and throw my arms over my head. Coach calls the strike, then asks. "What was *that* all about, Mr. Riggs?"

Jemmie stands and throws it to Ben. She picks up the bat. Before dropping back into a squat, she whispers, "Calm down, Big. It barely caught the outside corner."

I blink and look around, not sure what just happened to me. The fear was so bad it was a taste in my mouth. Ben takes a couple steps toward me off the mound. I wave him back. "A bug flew in my eye."

He stares at me for a second, then goes into his windup. I see the ball leave his hand. I swing as hard as I can, but when the bat clouts me in the back of the neck, it's pushing nothing but air. "Yer out!!!" hollers Coach as the ball thwacks Jemmie's glove. Leroy drops to his knees like he's been shot. The bell rings.

Coach tweets the twinky little whistle that hangs around his neck. "Blues win it four to three." And he sends us to the showers.

"Nice hit," says Leroy as he trots past me.

○

Jemmie and I stand in the hall, everyone but us rushing toward their next class. We both smell like deodorant. Jemmie's got little wet ringlets around her face again—but it doesn't make me melt the way it usually would. The message from Duane is between me and everything else.

"Let's go to the media center," she says. "Better check my e-mail before you hurt yourself."

"How?" I ask numbly. "We don't have Media until tomorrow morning."

She rolls her eyes. Butler is in the hall waiting for the last stragglers: us. Jemmie walks right up to him and tells him what's going on. She even pulls the paper out of her pack and makes him read it. "So, can we go to the media center, please?"

"Mr. Riggs may go. You need to stay here and further your education, Miss Lewis."

She looks at him like he's crazy. "You think I'd give him my password?"

Butler writes two passes. "You gotta know what button to push," she says as we hurry down the hall.

There are only three working computers in the media center; the other four have Out of Order signs taped to their screens with frowny faces on them. Kids are taking AR tests on the three that are operational.

We tell our story to Mrs. Buck, the media specialist. Trina Boyd is really put out that she has to surrender her computer. Jemmie says "Thank you, Trina" in the world's sweetest voice, but sticks her tongue out as Trina flounces away.

Jemmie types in the web address for AOL. "Come on, come on," I mutter, but it loads slowly. Finally the cursor blinks in the sign-on box. I'm too scared about what we might find out in a minute to pay attention to the password she types in. The news window opens.

Blip. Convoy ambushed after making wrong turn! Iraqis display bodies.

Blip. How long do you think the war will go on? A. Two to three weeks. B. Two to three months. C. Longer.

Blip. Bathing suit weather on its way! Three diets to get you ready for summer.

"Hurry up," Jemmie urges under her breath, but the AOL eye keeps spinning.

She finally gets into her mailbox and scrolls down. "There!" she whispers. "Second to last message. PFCRiggs22. If he's writing, he's got to be okay."

"Unless someone is typing for him."

She clicks on it, then slides out of the chair. I slide in.

Hey Jemmie,

   Sorry I used the S word in my last note. I'm not used to things going ka-boom! The whole thing was a false alarm. Some joker blew up one of the latrines. If they ever nail the guy who did it the sucker's going to pull some serious KP, maybe even face a court-martial. This isn't high school.

I hope you didn't scare the daylights out of my brother with the last note—he's kind of delicate.

Give Barf Boy this message from me: Everything is cool. I e-mailed Mom at work. I didn't mention my little scare. Don't tell her about it. It was no biggie but it might worry her.

BTW any luck with those tips I gave you???

Duane

I type back a message:

The latrine? How long can you hold it? Ha ha!
Don't worry I didn't tell Mom.
For your information your tips suck. And quit calling me Barf Boy. Stay safe.

Jus

"Would you say that latrine was taken out by friendly fire?" I ask as we walk slowly back to class.

She laughs, then touches one of the damp curls at the edge of her forehead. "Why are you staring? Is something wrong with my hair?"

"Who's staring? I'm not staring. Your hair is fine."

"Of course it is." She seems self-conscious as she runs her fingers over her cornrows. "Why did he call you Barf Boy?"

"Old story. I threw up in Mom's shoe when I was four. I don't even remember it, but Duane won't let me forget it."

"What were those tips he was talking about?"

Luckily we're at the door to the class. When we come into the room, everyone is writing. Ben glances up from his paper, worried—then he smiles. Guess he can still read me.

Not Butler. He looks back and forth from Jemmie to me.

When I give him the thumbs-up, Butler slaps a drumroll of joy on the edge of the desk.

Howdy Son,

Mom is mad at me—I understand that—but why you? You're picking Mom's side because you're around her all the time. I can just imagine what she says about me!

Trust me. The stuff that's going on between me and Mom goes two ways. It's not all my fault. But I shouldn't have to tell you that. You've seen her in action. I'm sorry you're in the middle of all this.

It sure would make me feel better if you'd talk to me when I call. Is that so hard? Just talk to me okay? I feel like I've lost both my sons.

Love,
Dad

Last bell is still ringing as I toss my books in my pack. I'm definitely going to study this weekend—Butler's isn't the only class I'm in danger of flunking—but for now, all I want to do is get to Jemmie's for my piano lesson.

I don't talk to her walking home, we're part of a crowd. Ben and Cass walk behind me bounce-passing a basketball. Cass is with us because the track coach, Mrs. Strickland, has a sick kid at home and had to cancel. Jemmie walks with Leroy a few steps ahead. Jemmie and I went through a lot together with Duane's message, but that was Monday, this is Friday. Since then it's like she's forgotten all about it.

With their long strides, she and Leroy have pulled away. As the distance grows, they look less like part of the group and more like a couple. It's okay. In ten minutes I'll be having a piano lesson with her. And Leroy? Leroy will be hanging out with *SpongeBob* and Jahmal.

I'm shrugging my shoulders to get the heavy pack to sit more comfortably when I see Leroy put his hand on Jemmie's back. "Illegal use of hands!" I blurt out before my brain can throw the switch. His hand slides off her back like touching her was an accident, but he glares at me over his shoulder.

I concentrate on the duct tape on my shoes and the sound of the ball. We'll be at her house soon.

"Heads up, Jus!" Ben calls. I ignore him. A pass I don't see coming bounces off my thigh.

I wish Ben would pass it to Leroy; the guy needs something

constructive to do with his hands. Five more minutes and we'll be at the Lewises'.

"Hey, Big?" Jemmie is walking backwards. "You mind if Leroy stays for your piano lesson?"

"Yeah," Leroy says. "I wanna learn too."

"What about the kid brother?" I say. "What if he burns down the house or something?"

"I can call him," he says.

"So, is it okay?" Jemmie asks. "I mean, you can say no." But I can tell she wants me to say yes.

"Go ahead, give Leroy his lesson. Give him my lesson too. I got plenty of other stuff to do. I'm going to be taking real lessons soon anyway." My face burns. Suddenly, it's hard to swallow. Good thing we're near my house. I sprint a few feet, the pack hitting my back. I turn in fast.

"Big?" she calls. "Hey, Big?" But she doesn't come after me. I know, because I wait behind the hedge.

"You heard the man," says Leroy. "He's got himself a new teacher. You're my teacher now." I listen until the twang of the ball fades away.

I slam the front door behind me and stand panting with my back against it. My heart feels like it's hanging off my chest like a loose button. I hate my life.

I take the stairs two at a time, shoulder the door, and stumble into the Duane Riggs Memorial Bedroom. Things will get better now. This is the refuge.

But the effect never kicks in. It's just a cruddy old room that smells like stale foot powder. Duane leers at me from the baseball trophy photo. *Piano lessons, Jus? You thought you could get next to a girl with piano lessons?*

"It beats making friends with her pet!" I reach for the picture but knock it over; Duane lands face down. For some reason this makes me madder. I snatch up the gold frame and bring the picture down hard on the corner of the dresser. The crunch of smashing glass sounds good.

There's some sparkly powder on the dresser corner, bits of crushed glass. I turn the picture over. "Oh, God..." I groan. Cracks radiate from a small hole over the middle of his chest. When it comes to bad juju, this must be the worst. It looks like he's just taken a bullet to the heart.

O

I've been comatose, rolled up in the sleeping bag for an hour when the Corolla coughs and dies in the driveway. I don't even open my eyes. All I want to do is stay mummy-wrapped with the Giz asleep on my chest, afloat in the Big Nothing.

I hear the front door open. "Justin?"

I don't move.

"Justin, are you home?"

I don't answer.

"Justin!" She sounds like I sound when she won't get out of bed—scared.

Giz complains with a loud *meow* as I wrestle my arms out of the bag and sit up."In Duane's room, Mom, doing homework. Be down in a sec." I throw the sleeping bag aside and climb out of bed.

"Mom?" I stop halfway down the stairs. "Are you okay?"

She clasps her purse to her chest. "Did you hear anything from Duane?"

"Not today."

"Me either." I can tell she needs a hug, but if I get close she'll look in my eyes and know how messed up I feel. She couldn't handle that. Because I can't hug her, I talk. "Duane's okay, Mom. He's fine. He's probably having himself a good old time. Hey, I have an idea. I'll take you out for supper. Not carryout, but sit-down. The whole deal."

"With Dad away we can't really afford—"

"My treat. You fly, I'll buy. If we go now, we can catch an Early Bird." I bolt up the stairs and toss the *Playboys* out of Duane's bottom drawer; I grab the twenties underneath and leave the magazines on the floor.

Mom is waiting in the kitchen with her purse on her knees. I flash Duane's twenties at her. "Where do you want to go? Sky's the limit."

"Where did *that* come from?"

"Duane's room. He said I could spend it. Where do you want to go?"

Decisions are hard for Mom when she's depressed, so I'm surprised when she answers right away. "Jim and Milt's."

"Great choice! The barbecue's spicy and the waitresses are hot." She swats my butt when I mention hot waitresses.

"Yow! You're not as wimpy as you used to be."

"No, I'm not," she says. I wonder if maybe there's a smashed picture of Dad in her room.

I offer her my arm. She takes it. It's Friday, date night USA, and I'm going out with my mother. Leroy would laugh if he knew but I don't care. Dad says I picked Mom's side, and he's right. I picked her side because she picked mine. She's the only one who has.

As soon as we walk into Jim and Milt's, Mom zeros in on a TV. There's one mounted in each corner of the room. Usually they're tuned to a sports station with a news crawl scrolling across the bottom. Tonight the war is being beamed at us from all corners. Mom lowers herself into a chair she's barely looked at. "Wait," I say. "I have a better idea. Let's do Chinese."

We end up at the China Super Buffet on Monroe. No TVs there. We sip green tea. Since we don't know how to use them, we stab things with our chopsticks. The waiter brings us forks. I get us a couple of Cokes. Mom is smiling.

I'm glad she's having a good time. I would be too, except I keep getting flashes of Leroy and Jemmie on the piano bench. In most of them, no one's playing the piano.

I wrap a chunk of duck in a napkin for the Giz. The next thing on the schedule is probably a long night on the sofa parked in front of the war. I check out the bill and do a little subtraction. "Hey, Mom. How about a movie?" Even with the tip, I have enough for tickets.

We drive to the multiplex at the mall. Mom insists I choose the movie since I'm paying. "How thoughtful!" she says when I pick a romantic comedy over action-adventure. "You're going to make some lucky girl a great date."

"Oh, yeah," I say, stuffing my two bucks' change in my pocket. "Right after the face transplant."

"What's wrong with your face? I like your face!"

"Half the time it looks like I fell asleep on a fire ant mound."

"You're too self-conscious, Justin. Dad's skin was much worse when he was your age."

"No way. He looks good in all his kid pictures."

"Do you think your father would keep a picture that made him look less than perfect?" She checks her watch. "We have half an hour before the show starts. Let's get you some new sneakers. You could use a pair."

"Yeah?" I say, lifting a taped shoe. "Ya think?"

We walk by the pet store. I remember Jemmie with the ferret sticking out of the neck of her sweatshirt. It chokes me up.

Mom picks the shoes. I'm not that interested. I wear the new shoes out of the store, but carry the old pair in a box under my arm. "Go on," Mom says, pointing out a trash can. "Make a deposit."

"No, I think I'll keep them."

"What do you plan to do, give them a decent burial?"

"I kind of like them, Mom. I'm used to them."

Mom threads her arm through mine. "You're the most loyal person I know, Jus."

"Because I'm true to my shoes?"

She squeezes my arm. "It's not just the shoes—you're loyal to everything and everybody."

Dad would disagree. So would Ben; even Duane, if he could see the smashed picture. "I'm loyal to you, Mom."

"And I'm loyal to you." We're beginning to sound like a bad sitcom, but that doesn't keep the middle of my chest from glowing like the wires in a toaster.

"This is getting way too feel-good. Let's go find seats."

Inside the theater Mom makes a beeline for a middle row— which is fine. I don't have to be super-close to the screen when I watch people kiss. As I fall into my seat, she ruffs the back of my hair. "Mo-om!"

Suddenly I remember her doing the same thing a long time ago. I'm sitting in a movie theater with the whole family. Mom and Dad hold hands. Duane stuffs popcorn down my T-shirt. I lift myself up and down on the chair arms to make the seat squeak. Mom reaches over and ruffs the back of my hair. For a second I remember what it felt like to be that dumb little kid. He took the whole family thing for granted. He thought it was going to last.

I'm relieved when the lights start to dim. Mom and I both need a couple of hours of an out-of-body experience.

I turn toward the front of the theater, ready to fade, and I see them. Not their faces, just the backs of their heads, their matching cornrows, but it's obviously Leroy and Jemmie seated front row, center. What did she say when the two of us sat in the same exact spot to watch Saruman's evil orcs?

Best seats in the house, Big.

○

When we get home, Mom is smiling, re-running the movie in her head. She doesn't notice that something's wrong. She believes me when I tell her I'm tired. She even lets me use the bathroom first.

I brush my teeth, but don't bother with the face-scrub routine—who looks at my face anyway? I avoid Duane's and head for my own bedroom. To excavate the bed I push the dirty laundry over the side, then pry off my new sneaks. I add my shirt to the pile on the floor and let my jeans accordion around my feet. I crash-land on top of the covers and hit the switch on the bedside light.

I don't remember much about the movie, but I can see the shapes of their two heads against the screen perfectly. Bet they were holding hands. Bet he asked her to the next dance. My eyes sting and my nose floods with snot. *You're pathetic,* says Duane. I tell him to get out of my room.

The darkness feels thick, almost like it's trying to suffocate me. I sit up in bed and listen. Mom flushed the toilet a while ago—I haven't heard a thing since. I grope for the light switch.

I pull my dirty shirt over my head and step into my jeans. Downstairs. I turn the TV on low and zap CNN off the screen. One channel away a guy in a white hat is making an omelet. It reminds me of eating breakfast at Jemmie's house.

The air is hard to breathe here too. Maybe it's the house.

I desert the French chef and let myself out the front door quietly.

I should go back and get my shoes. The porch floor is as cold as the metal benches in the school locker room. But I don't want to go back; in a while I'll get used to it. I cut across the damp grass. The ladder is still on the ground propped against the house, right where Duane, Ben, and I left it two summers ago. I have to pull hard to disentangle it from the witch grass that has grown through the rungs.

It's a struggle to lift and walk the ladder up on one end. I lose control. It crashes against the edge of the roof. I hold my breath and wait for a light to come on inside but nothing happens. I'm on the opposite side of the house from Mom's room, so I guess she didn't hear. I wiggle the aluminum ladder around until the feet seem stable. Even fully extended, the ladder is barely tall enough to reach. I remember that Duane held the bottom for Ben and me.

I put a foot on the first rung and start to climb. With each step the ladder feels less steady. The *wah-wah* as it bends in and out gets worse. I stop just outside the window of the Duane Riggs Memorial Bedroom hoping the shimmy in the ladder will settle down. I look through the window and almost fall off. For a second the sleeping bag heaped on the bed is Duane, curled up on his side.

When I finally make it to the top, I throw my arms over the edge and lie splayed like a starfish. My chest and arms are on the roof, my feet on the ladder. I'm trying to get a knee up when I hear—and feel—the ladder judder along the edge of the roof. It slides until the only thing that keeps it from falling is my left big toe.

I hang, suspended between the roof and the ladder, afraid to breathe, afraid to move.

And then my shirt begins to ride up. The skin on my stomach burns as I slide slowly toward the drop-off. If I don't do something I'll fall two stories.

I claw the rough shingles with my fingernails. Still sliding, I direct every bit of strength in my body to my left big toe and the leg that's attached to it, and I pull. With a squeal, the ladder straightens.

Both feet on the ladder and my chest on the roof, I suck in deep breaths and listen to the ocean of blood in my ears. My legs shake.

I crawl onto the roof exhausted and sprawl flat on my back, a splat of kid.

After all I've been through I expect a few stars. But clouds form a lid over the neighborhood. "This is it?" I groan. "This is the best you could do?" The stars were perfect the night Duane, Ben, and I camped up here. Nothing's perfect these days, and anything that used to be seems to have a great big crack down the middle now.

I crawl on hands and knees to the roof peak and sit. The ridge dents my butt. My teeth chatter, my feet are numb. I look down on my neighborhood. Over that way, Jemmie is in her bed. And over there Leroy is in his—and they're dreaming about each other.

I thought I was sneaking up on her. I thought she sort of liked me. "Are you kidding?" I say out loud. "Jemmie Lewis like *you*? Never has, never will."

Dear Duane,

It's two in the morning, so I guess it's Saturday. I just did a remake of the Ben-Duane-Justin roof scene only this time I was solo. The ladder slipped on the way up and I about killed myself. After all that trouble there weren't any stars. That's the way things are going these days. Tell me again why you joined the Army? And don't leave out why you couldn't hold off a few years—like 'til I could go with you.

Mom's doing better. I keep her halfway happy at least half of the time. It's me who's messed up. It might help to talk—but who to? Ben doesn't have time and Mom would only go into a slump. I think I'm getting high blood pressure.

Forget Jemmie. I'm never mentioning her again and I'd appreciate it if you didn't either. Just so you know, she's going with Leroy.

Justin

P.S. Those guys who paid money for your famous girl-getting tips were robbed.

The last thing I remember is the woman on the cooking channel making lasagna.

A scraping sound wakes me up. It's not on the TV, which, strangely, is off. I look over the side of the chair and there's the remote with its guts spilled. Guess I knocked it off the arm in my sleep.

I listen hard but don't hear anything. The window over the TV is turning gray; it's starting to get light out. My eyes close. I've about decided I dreamed up the noise when the front door rattles.

My eyes pop open. Someone is breaking in! I jump out of the chair to call 911—but they'd get here too late to do anything but put up crime-scene tape and chalk my outline on the floor.

I sprint to the kitchen but ignore the phone. Instead I grab a chair to jam under the knob. It always works in cop shows.

I'm a few feet from the door when the knob turns. As the door swings open, I sweep the chair up and hold it over my head.

"Damn," says Dad, staring at the chair. "Put that down before you hurt yourself, son." My knees are shaking, the chair is shaking—but it's like electricity is shooting through my body. My muscles stay locked. "Good work defending the old homestead," he adds, "but everything's okay. You can put the chair down."

"Why are you here?"

"I live here, remember?" He spreads his arms. "Hey, Jack is back!"

I bring the chair down so hard it smashes against the floor.

"Damn," Dad repeats, watching a chair leg roll across the rug. "Bet that relieved a lot of stress. Mind if I come in?"

All that's left in my hand is the thick wooden slat from the top of the chair. I hold it like a sword. "Yes. I *do* mind."

He eases a tan suitcase through the door, followed by a brown one, but keeps both feet on the porch. His hands slide into his pants pockets. He jingles his change and keys. "So, what do we do now?"

"Is Mom expecting you?"

Wearing an embarrassed grin, he says, "Not really. I thought I'd surprise her. Now, would you drop the weapon?" He steps inside and spreads his arms again, like I missed the cue the first time. "Come on son, I need a hug."

I grip the piece of chair. "Go back to Atlanta, Dad. Mom and I are fine."

Dad's air-hug wilts. "Listen," he says, "I know you're angry—"

"Yeah? How would you know that? How would you know anything about me?"

"Okay, okay." He hides behind an arm as if I'm going to hit him, then peers over it. "We have a lot of catching up to do. We'll talk about anything you want for as long as you want later—but right now I'm bushed. I've been on the road for hours. I need a shower, and I have to talk to Mom. You know I'll need my strength for that." He winks at me. "Between you and me, she's going to hand me my head."

I point the broken slat at him. "Forget Mom. If you don't get out of here, *I'll* hand you your head!"

Dad whistles between his teeth. "You've developed some

backbone while I've been away, that's for sure. Good for you, son. You needed a little."

He takes two steps toward me, but I fall back. "Why did you do it, Dad? Why did you mess around? Mom loves you!"

He rubs the side of his neck. "You know, I could handle this better with a cup of coffee in me."

"I stuck up for you, Dad! Always! I told Mom she was imagining things and the whole time you were screwing around, letting other women smear lipstick on your clothes." I hurl the words at him; spit flies. It scares me how mad I am.

He slips off his jacket but seems to have second thoughts about hanging it up. If this were a sales call, he'd leave his card and head for the nearest exit. He looks toward the door, then back at me. "I know I let you down, son, and I'm sorry. God, this is hard," he mutters. "I never thought I'd be apologizing to my own kid. What I did was wrong, but you'll understand when you get older. Sometimes things just happen."

"Things don't just happen—you *let* them happen. You *make* them happen."

"Okay, okay, you're right. But they won't happen anymore. I swear." He opens his hands as if he's showing me he's unarmed and takes another step toward me. "So, what do you say? Will you let me stick around?"

"Why should I?"

"Because I'm a fun guy? Because you missed me? Uhhh...because I let you pick the toppings when we order pizza?"

This is what Dad does, he puts things over on people by making them laugh. I don't even smile.

"Okay...how about something practical? Let me stay and I'll pay the bills. They must be piling up pretty bad."

"I already paid them."

There's a pause while that sinks in. "You know how to write a check?"

"It isn't that hard. By the way, you should keep a current balance."

"Good tip." But he's turned his attention to something behind me; I look too. Mom is standing on the stairs. She's almost as pale as her white terry robe; she doesn't smile. I expect her to dissolve into tears. I feel proud of her when she doesn't. She's developed a little backbone too.

Dad exhales slowly and then walks to the foot of the stairs. The Units watch each other like a couple of dogs that don't know whether to sniff butts or start a fight.

I stand beside him, like I'm choice A and he's choice B. "We don't need him, Mom. We'll be okay. I'll get a part-time job."

Dad puts a foot on the first stair, his hand on the banister, edging closer to her. "Can't we talk things over, Kathy? We've been married twenty-two years. Just give me twenty minutes. That's less than one minute for each year, what do you say?"

"Don't do it, Mom. He'll talk you into something you don't want to do."

He pretends I'm not here. He concentrates on Mom. I can't kick him out; she can. But Mom turns to me. Her eyes probe mine, then she faces Dad and folds her arms. "Justin's right. We can get along without you, Jack. We have been. Jus has done a great job while you were off running around. He took care of things. He's reliable." When he hears the word *reliable*, Dad flinches. She hasn't raised her voice or burst into tears, but for once he's listening.

"I don't like the example you set for our boys," she continues. "I don't want Justin or Duane to treat women the way you do." Then softer, she says, "I don't like myself when I'm with you. I yell and I cry; I'm always the victim."

"Come on, Kathy." In a quick move he reaches out and captures her hand. "I know I've been a lousy husband, but everything's going to be all right. I guarantee it."

I feel myself flicker like a flame going out. They've forgotten I'm here. "Is that the one-year guarantee, or the five?" I say loudly as he squeezes her hand. "And can we get it in writing? We want to read the fine print."

"Justin—"

"What, Dad? You don't like my tone? Mom and I both see what you're doing. You're weaseling your way back in!"

He lifts an eyebrow. "Watch yourself, son. You're about to cross the line."

"Mom? Want me to throw him out?"

Mom smiles at me apologetically. "Leave us alone for a little while. Okay?" I realize he's still holding her hand.

"Fine! Talk! Let me know what you two decide."

The box with my old sneakers in it is on the coffee table. I toss the lid on the floor and jam my feet into them. I remember to grab a sweatshirt this time. I may be gone a while.

On the porch I pull the shirt over my head. When I look out into the yard I see that the world ends at the azalea hedge. Everything else has been erased by a heavy mist. Water droplets hang on every ratty blade of grass in the yard. My sneaks are soaked before I make it to the road.

As I stride away the world stays small, like a bubble that travels with me. Things appear and disappear: a mailbox, a bike on a lawn, a recycle bin. Edges are soft, and the world has no color.

Everyone I know is in bed. I don't want to see them anyway.

As I pace the neighborhood I think, here's *Casablanca*, Dad style: Ilsa flies away and Rick hooks up with the first girl who walks into his bar. The problem is, Rick wouldn't do it. I know he wouldn't. He'd watch the door pretty much forever, hoping Ilsa would come back.

I'm on Jemmie's street when I hear the quiet creak of chains. I follow the sound; I can't help myself. If it's Jemmie on the porch swing I'm going to ask her why she picked Leroy. Screw Duane's advice about not spilling. What have I got to lose?

I stop a few feet from the porch steps when I see who it is. "Oh, hi."

Nana Grace cradles a cup of coffee in her hands and pushes the swing gently with her toes. Her eyes are on the sky. I wonder what she's looking at—the mist is still pretty thick. "What kind of day you think we got coming?" she asks.

I drag myself up the steps and fall into the seat beside her. "Lousy."

"You think so? I see a little pink where the sun is nibblin' at the mist over there. I bet all this mess is gonna burn off and we'll have ourselves a beautiful day."

"My dad came home."

"Good…good." She nods once. "So you're out walkin'?"

"He and Mom are negotiating. He comes back and all of a sudden I'm, like, extra."

"Not extra—they just got things to talk about."

"And I don't?"

"Sure you do, but this ain't the time. They gotta talk first."

"What should I do? Get in line, take a number?"

"Be patient. You'll get your chance."

"It doesn't matter anyway. Nothing's going to change. Things will be fine for a while, then he'll go on a trip and Mom'll get jealous and there goes the cease-fire. When it was just Mom and me, things were regular. We don't need him."

"Folks change, Justin. Sinners become saints. You need to give your father a chance. You can't just toss family away."

"I only want to toss Dad. Mom, I'll keep."

She runs her palm along the sleeve of my sweatshirt. "Afraid you don't get to pick and choose. Family is family." She pushes herself to her feet and leans over the porch rail. "Now, see over there? That sky is colorin' up nice."

"I think I'll walk some more."

"Walkin's good."

I want the mist to get so thick no one can see me at all: Justin the shadow man. I walk a block and turn. I can still see Nana Grace and the porch. Like she said, it's burning off, and the neighborhood is waking up.

At Leroy's, Jahmal is in the yard tossing a plastic ball into the air and swinging a bat at it. "Hey, Justin. Pitch me, okay?"

"I'm busy. Get Leroy to pitch you."

"Can't. He's cleaning the bathroom." Jahmal pushes up the super-long sleeves of his brother's Tupac jacket. Leroy would kill him if he knew he was wearing it. I wouldn't want it to get real messed up, but a little mud on the sacred jacket would be okay.

"You don't *look* busy." Jahmal tosses the ball, takes another swipe at it, and hits it.

"Well, I am." The ball is about to pop me in the chest, so I catch it. I turn it over in my fingers. It's big as a grapefruit and practically weightless. It matches the yellow plastic bat on his shoulder. "All right, I'll pitch you a couple. Ya ready?"

Like Leroy, Jahmal has to position his feet, wiggle his butt, wave the bat around. "Less show, more go," I tell him and I toss it at him. The kid whips the bat so hard he wrings himself out. Legs crossed, he almost falls down, but the ball skips over the top of the bat.

I trot after it and scoop it up just before it goes down a storm drain.

"Saw you at the movies last night," he says, turning to face me in my new spot.

My heart starts acting funny. "Yeah? Where were you sitting?"

He has to do the whole bat-wave, butt-wiggle thing before he can answer. "Front row. Leroy and me were on a date with Jemmie."

I'm thinking like crazy. I didn't see Jahmal, but he's kind of short—and who looks for a brother on a date? I throw the ball. He swats it back. "So, you went on a date with Jemmie? Did you hold her hand?"

Jahmal lets the bat tip drop and gives me a *duh* look. "No way. She has girl germs. Besides, Jemmie kept both hands on the bucket of popcorn the whole time." He brightens. "She bought me Gummi Bears."

"Sounds like a hot time: you ate Gummi Bears and you dodged a case of girl germs... How about your brother, did Jemmie give him any girl germs? Did he have a good time?"

Jahmal shrugs. "He said the movie was lame. When we got home he yelled at Mom. She gave him extra Saturday work."

Jahmal pops up the next pitch I lob his way. I tip my head and watch the yellow ball sail up into a sky that is suddenly blue. They didn't hold hands and Leroy came home mad.

Sweet.

I pitch to Jahmal for a good half hour—then his Mom calls him in to do his Saturday work. "See ya, Lard," he says in a pipsqueak version of Leroy's voice.

I yell after him, "That's *Mr.* Lard to you." But I'm not mad. Things are looking up.

○

Dad's Town Car's been gone so long that for a second it looks like an alien spacecraft in the driveway. But as I stare, his latest absence begins to blend with all the other times he's left and come back. It's not exactly the same though. I know things about Dad I didn't know before. I wish I could un-know them.

I walk to the front door, but stop without opening it. Country music drains out around the edges like old bathwater.

"Sounds like your dad is home," says Mr. Barnett, who's walking by with Killer and Lillian. "God, he has awful taste."

"Yeah," I agree. "The worst." And I let myself in.

Dad's in the kitchen wearing Mom's Kiss the Cook apron, frying a whole pound of bacon. Mom must've forgotten to tell him we've been trying to eat healthier.

He's facing away and doesn't see me standing in the kitchen door. His bald head reflects the sun through the window. It reminds me of the moon in the model solar system he helped me build for science fair.

He whistles along with the radio and flips slices of bacon.

Nana Grace says people change. Not from what I've seen. Not Dad, anyway. But if there's a chance—even if it's only a lottery chance—I feel like I should give it to him. Family is family.

Dear Duane,

Jack is back. He showed up a week ago acting like nothing happened, but Mom wouldn't let him get away with it—she's tired of his crap. If he says something sarcastic she points to the door. But most of the time he's nice to her—and she's nice back.

In fact, the Units are so considerate it's like it isn't even them. They talk about the past a lot. Not the bad parts—just the warm and fuzzy stuff. I think they wish they could go back and try again.

If you're not busy getting shot at or anything dig some change out of your pocket and call, okay??? Since Mom and Dad are all big on the past I've heard a few interesting stories from when you were a kid. What good is hearing embarrassing stuff if I can't get on you about it?

Justin

Nana Grace answers the door with spaghetti sauce on her apron. "Come on in," she says, "but don't expect a lot of conversation. I'm makin' lasagna for forty."

"Why?"

"The girls have their first meet this afternoon. The team spirit dinner's right after."

"I saw them get on the bus. Jemmie isn't going to run, is she?"

"No, she says she's gonna cheer the team, but you know sittin' on the sidelines cheerin' ain't her style. She's been feelin' pretty blue." She holds the door for me. "Why don't you come to the team dinner? You always make her smile."

"You think she'd want me to?"

"Sure, you'd be a nice surprise."

Surprise, yes, but nice? I take a step back from the open door. If I'm going to a dinner with Jemmie, I need a shower more than I need to practice. Not that going's definite. I have to check the face. I'm about to make an excuse and go when I remember the stolen music notebook in my pack. "I can play a little while—but I have stuff to do for Mom." Which is completely not true. After work the Units have an appointment with a marriage counselor, Mom's idea.

"Play a little then. I been looking forward to hearin' that song you been makin' up."

As soon as she's in the kitchen I stuff the notebook under the rest of the music in the bench. I play "Sweet Jemmie," but never really get into it. I keep thinking about the dinner and whether or not I should go. "I'm leaving now, Nana Grace."

"See you tonight, then. Come by the school around six."

"Yeah. If I get my other stuff done."

O

Dad is straightening his necktie when I walk in, but he grabs the end and raises it over his head like a hanging rope. His eyes cross.

"Go on, Dad. You'll be okay. It's only a counseling appointment. All you have to do is talk."

"Talk," he says. "I'm good at that." He smooths the tie carefully. "Listen, I might take Mom out for supper after the appointment. Are you okay with that?" He's never asked me before. Asking must be part of the new considerate Dad.

"Sure. Fine with me. I might be out too. There's a team spirit dinner at the school."

He wiggles his eyebrows. "Ah, yes. The lovely Jemmie Lewis." I could kill Mom for ratting me out—now he's going to ride me. But he doesn't. He's too worried about his own girl problems. "Dead man walking...," he announces, and heads for the door.

I take a shower, then study the face in the bathroom mirror. To show up at the dinner or not to show—that is the question. Examination of the face proves inconclusive: small outbreak on forehead, but no major eruptions in progress.

It's only four-fifteen. I pace around the house, drumming on everything with my palms, but pacing feels too slow. I jog the stairs and trot up and down the hall. I almost iron another T-shirt, then remember Jemmie in her cruddy old sweatshirt when we went to the movies. Better keep it casual.

I bound up the stairs for the thirteenth time, then grab the bar mounted in Duane's door. I do a chin-up. Am I getting stronger? *You sure are*, says the voice of Duane. *You're sweating like a horse, bro.*

I take another shower, put on more pit-stop and a clean but unironed T-shirt, one that says "Beware! The Flying Hamsters of Doom Are at Hand!" My only other choice has the Wild Adventures Theme Park logo on the pocket.

After the shower I visit the Duane Riggs Memorial Bedroom and resurrect my brother's old hair dryer from a bottom drawer. I don't normally use one, but if I can get the hair to dry in the upright position it might add half an inch to my height. I need that half inch.

As I comb and blow hot air at my head, Duane and Lisi smile at me from their prom picture. Mom thought *I* was glowing? She should take a look at her number-one son and his girlfriend—especially the girlfriend.

What is it that gets a girl to light up like that? It's got to be more than telling her she has pretty eyes or making friends with her pet.

Maybe it's that thing Mom calls "chemistry." Look what chemistry did for Fred Astaire, a dweeb with a few good moves. Look what it did for Bogart, all crusty and five o'clock shadowy on the *African Queen*.

But chemistry is something you either have or you don't. Dad has it. Duane has it. I swivel on the balls of my feet to face the mirror, checking for chemistry. Forget it. It's easy to see that I don't have it.

Plus, the hair looks really stupid. I put my head under the faucet and comb the hair flat. Flat is worse—and now my shirt and the front of my pants are soaked. I turn slowly, watching myself in the mirror. I look bad from every angle.

I fall onto Duane's bed. For a couple of seconds, the springs reverberate with the shock. Then everything gets real still.

I see myself running wind sprints up and down the stairs; I remember feeling like Mr. Universe after one lousy chin-up. I was excited for a while there, thinking I was going to the dinner, but what would be the point?

The phone beside the bed rings. I jump. Then I do a Duane. He never answered on the first ring. If it wasn't for him, why bother? If it was, it was probably a girl, so why act anxious? I let it ring again.

As the phone rings a third time, I reach over slowly and pick it up. "Yeah?"

The line seems dead. I'm about to hang up when there's a burst of static, and then a voice. "Jus! Can you hear me?"

"Duane!" I sit straight up. "Where are you? How are you? Are you alive and everything?"

"Whoa, one question at a time. I only have about five minutes. Long story short, I'm fine. I don't know what's on the tube, but when you see those tanks rolling through Baghdad, I'm not on 'em. Wish I was, the war's going great."

"You keep your butt right where it is," I tell him.

"What, and miss the whole thing sitting on the bench? Sorry—there I go with the baseball crap again." His voice trails off. "I miss you guys."

"We miss you too. Hey, Dad came home."

"Took him long enough."

"Yeah, he set a new record. You know, you never answered my question. Did he always mess around, or was this, like, the first time?"

A long silence, then, "No, it wasn't the first time. It doesn't happen as often as Mom thinks, but it happens."

"Why didn't you tell me?"

"I didn't want to know about it myself. Why make you feel

bad? Besides, Dad's a good guy in other ways. We'll talk when I get home. The clock's ticking. Are the Units there?"

"No. They're seeing a marriage counselor. Mom insisted."

He laughs. "She'll nail his butt down yet. Listen, tell 'em I'm okay. Tell Mom to stand down in the worry department. I don't have my fingers crossed or anything, things are really okay. I'll try to e-mail her tomorrow. Now, Jus, tell the doctor about your love life. Sounds like it needs immediate first aid."

He has five minutes and he wants to hear about my love life. "Long story short? It stinks," and I give it to him in the quick form, ending with the dinner I'm not going to.

"And why aren't you going?"

"Why? For one thing I look like dog crap. And for another she didn't invite me, her grandmother did. What if I get there and she's with Leroy?"

"And what if she isn't?"

"She probably doesn't even want me to come. What if I get there and she looks bad-surprised to see me?"

"Then you get embarrassed. Big deal. At least you get a free meal out of it."

"Forget the free meal. If she's bad-surprised, I'm coming home."

"There's a hitch in your coming-home plan, bro."

"Yeah, what's that?"

"First you gotta get there."

There's a bunch of clicking at the other end of the line and the phone goes dead. "Okay!" I yell into the receiver, "I'll go, but if this is a mistake you're seriously dead, Duane."

I leave a note for the Units. They're going to feel bad they missed talking to Duane. Mom will want to know every word of the five-minute call when I get back.

Maybe I'll tell them it only lasted thirty seconds.

I hit the cool outside air. I feel my wet scalp pucker; but at the same time I'm sweating. As I walk, I fan my shirt in and out to disperse smells. Wish I'd checked the mirror again. My hair is probably doing something strange.

A few cars are parked in front of the school, volunteers for the team spirit dinner. Ben is on the basketball court shooting hoops by himself. "Hey, Jus! What are you doing here?"

"Nothing. You?"

"Waiting for the team to come back from the meet." He passes me the ball. We trade a couple of easy shots, then Ben picks up the tempo.

Problem: If I don't play hard I look like a wimp; if I do I sweat. I tell him about Duane's call, at least the parts about being okay. That slows the action for a while, then Ben really turns it on.

If Jemmie doesn't get here soon I'll be nothing but a collection of bad smells.

O

Ben's on the free-throw line when the bus pulls up. From a window near the front, Cass leans across Jemmie and waves wildly. Ben tosses me the ball and sprints away. He arrives just in time to catch Cass when she leaps off the top step.

I give the ball a couple of slow bounces. I notice that I'm standing at the center of my own personal cloud of deodorant and sweat. Who knows what weird position my hair dried in. Time to head home.

But as the rest of the team swarms off the bus, one girl is left behind. Doesn't anyone see Jemmie, sitting there looking all abandoned? I wave. She doesn't see me. She stares straight ahead.

When she finally climbs off the bus, she stands by herself a few feet from the knot of girls who bounce up and down as they tell Ben about the meet. It's easy to see that they won, and that Cass had a lot to do with it.

I've got to cheer Jemmie up. No one else is going to do it. Didn't Nana Grace say I always make her smile?

I wave again. This time she sees me. She turns on her heel and walks past the crowd, then stops. She looks back at the team. Maybe she saw how bad my hair looks and changed her mind about coming over. But then, in a rush, she sprints the rest of the way to the basketball court.

She doesn't say hello, she just claps her hands and holds them open, like, gimme the ball, sucker.

"You want this ball," I tell her. "Come and get it." I fake like I'm going to keep it away from her, then shoot it at her, loop de loop, from behind my back.

With her bad leg she can't maneuver like she used to. The ball gets past her and rolls into the fence.

"My fault—sorry."

She stares after it, then walks slowly over and picks it up. She glances at the basket but doesn't take a shot. Instead, she tucks the ball into her side and walks up to me. Holding the ball against her hip with one arm, she slings her other arm around my neck. "Glad you're here, Big."

"Ben and I were shooting a few hoops…"

The arm around my neck tightens. "Come on. Nana probably needs help setting things up for the dinner." As we pass the cluster of girls, Jemmie yells, "Here's your ball, Ben," and flips it into the middle of the crowd.

○

When we reach the cafetorium, Cass's mother is putting the last centerpiece—a sneaker with a jelly jar of flowers in it—on the last table. "How did it go, Jemmie?" Mrs. Bodine wipes her damp hands on her apron.

"You should've been there." Jemmie smiles big. "Cass was great! She'll tell you about it herself when she gets out of the shower, but she was the best."

"Really? Oh my." Mrs. Bodine's freckled cheeks flush. She seems surprised and a little embarrassed by the good news. "They're back," she calls, retreating into the kitchen. "It sounds as if they did okay."

Jemmie and I stand there. We have the whole cafetorium to ourselves.

"You think they need some help in there?" I ask.

"No. They're fine." She isn't smiling anymore.

"Then what do you want to do?"

When she doesn't answer, I pull out a chair. "Here, sit." I nudge the backs of her knees with the seat, but they refuse to bend. "Okay, don't sit. What do you want to do?"

"I want to explode!" she wails, collapsing into the chair.

"Be my guest. But would you mind stepping away from the table? Everything looks so pretty." I don't even get a smile. "That was a joke…you explode…you mess up the table."

Tears well in her eyes.

"The joke wasn't *that* bad."

Her eyelashes look wet. "I can't stand it any more. When those other girls were running—I wanted to run so bad. I cheered for Cass. I wanted her to win, only…"

"You wanted to win yourself."

She bites her lip and nods. "She even won the hundred meters." Her voice gets hoarse. "That's my race."

"It'll be your race again."

"When? Tell me when, Big."

"I don't know. Soon?" But it's like guessing when Duane will

231

come home. "It's going to have a happy ending," I assure her.

"Yeah? What kind of happy ending?"

"Let's see… If this was one of my mom's old movies—"

"Like one with Hitler in a funny hat?"

"Okay, but then it'll be in black and white."

"That works." She snuffs loudly, then puts her arm next to mine. "I'm black, you're white."

"So far so good. Uh…you want me in the movie?"

"Maybe." She puts her elbows on her knees and rests her chin in her hands. "So, what happens in my movie?"

"In your movie—starring you, of course—there's this girl named Jemmie Lewis, who runs."

"Best in the school," she adds.

"Right. I forgot to mention that. Best anywhere." I pull out a chair and sit too. "Listen, do you want Leroy in the movie? Leading man, or something like that? I mean, he's really, really, really—"

She cuts me off. "Yeah, he's cute but he brags too much. Get back to the part about running."

"He *brags* too much?"

She rolls her eyes. "He goes on about himself all the time. Girls don't like that."

"No kidding?" I wonder if Duane knows about this.

"So, what happens in my movie?"

"Oh yeah, like I said, Jemmie Lewis is the world's best runner—until she gets injured."

She blows out, exasperated. "This is too much like real life."

"But hold it, it doesn't end there."

"What happens?"

"The injury is bad, but it heals—slowly.

"Slowly? This is a crappy movie!"

"It *has* to heal slowly—to build suspense. The movie ends with a gold medal in the Olympics."

"For the hundred meters?" Her eyes come alive.

"Yeah, the hundred meters. She beats her friend Cass Bodine by an eyelash."

"I *do* have longer eyelashes. But is this, like, years later?"

"Not too many years."

The light in her eyes goes out. To Jemmie "years later" and "never" are the same thing.

"All good movies are like that," I explain quickly. "Things have to be lousy before they get better."

"Like life." She wipes her nose on her sleeve—another thing a girl wouldn't do around a guy she liked. "But what does Jemmie Lewis do while she can't run?"

"She hangs out with her friends." Her eyes fill with tears; she's thinking of Cass. I want to wave my arms and shout, hey, I'm right here. But she's blind when it comes to me.

And I wonder, what would Humphrey Bogart do? I don't have a clue. But whatever he did it would work, because he's confident—women trust him. Like Ilsa says to him in *Casablanca*, "You'll have to think for both of us!"

Trying to think for both of us, I look wildly around and see the piano on the stage. "Come with me. I want to play you something."

"You mean like music?"

"Yeah, let's use that piano up there." I grab her hands and lift her out of the chair. I let go of one hand but not the other and walk her toward the stage. I take big strides. She squeezes my hand as she trots to keep up.

I may act confident, but this is the stupidest thing I've ever done. There aren't any people in the cafetorium at this moment, but mothers are spooning fruit cocktail into plastic bowls one wall away, and cool girls who smell like shampoo and mousse are about to converge on this room.

For a second I'm paralyzed by the magnitude of my stupid

move. What am I doing? Jemmie won't be lifting weights or wandering around the living room. I'm making her listen to me play an actual performance. What if I choke?

Bogart wouldn't choke. In the clutch he would sit down and play, even if he didn't know how.

And I know how.

I uncover the keyboard. The keys grin up at me. It's not like I'm alone. It's me and Mr. Baldwin.

I start out softly. With the lid that covers the strings down, "Sweet Jemmie" is quiet and muffled, and not quite there.

Jemmie stands with her elbows on the piano lid. Her eyes are closed. She looks desolate. Her lashes—which really *are* long—are wet with tears. Would it make a difference if she knew this song was hers? Bogart would tell her—in a totally cool and casual way—and she'd pass out with joy. But I'm not Bogart. So I let the music talk.

Her eyes stay closed, but as the notes beat softly, like rain, on the underside of the lid, the corners of her mouth begin to turn up. She looks like she's in the middle of a good dream.

I hit the last note thinking she'll wake up now and everything will be the same as before. Eyes still closed, she says softly, "Play it again, Big."

"Wait. I gotta do something."

A warm, dusty smell escapes from the dark interior of the piano. The felt hammers are poised above the strings. I have the lid up, but I can't figure out how to make it stay that way. I can't ask Jemmie to hold it. "Uhhh…"

Her eyes flutter open. She ducks under and raises a wooden bar that slots into the lid. "Just like the hood of a car," she says.

"Right. Thanks." I slide the bench so she can sit beside me. "You want to ride shotgun?"

Our shoulders brush as I strike the first chord. My chord

fills the dusty corners of the stage. It rolls across the folding tables and into the hall.

It's the best sound I've ever heard, and I'm the one who's making it. I play louder.

If this were a movie the guy at the piano would still be playing as the credits rolled and the lights came up. Moviegoers would shuffle out to the parking lot, but the guy playing the piano and the girl sitting with him would never leave the moment.

I'm coming to the end again; the piece begins to fade out like when I played it for Butler—the way her father did in "Sweet Leona." Marvin and me, we're guys with full hearts and low expectations. At least we don't brag.

But this time the sad ending is wrong—it's not the one Jemmie needs. I change the fingering here and there and shift to a major key. Happy and sad are that close together.

I reach the new end—the real end. But the last note isn't the last sound. The last sound is Jemmie's whisper: "Wow, Big. That was beautiful."

In a second the cafetorium will be full of runners, speech makers, and the clatter of forks, but right now it's just Jemmie and me.

Bogart wouldn't waste this moment. Heck, Duane Riggs wouldn't waste it.

What have I got to lose?

"Glad you like it." I toss the next words at her. "I wrote it for you."

5/10

The Helen Kate Furness
Free Library
Wallingford, Pennsylvania   19086

GAYLORD M